Revenge of the Cheerleaders

Also by Janette Rallison

Playing the Field
All's Fair in Love, War, and High School
Life, Love, and the Pursuit of Free Throws
Fame, Glory, and Other Things on My To Do List
It's a Mall World After All

Revenge *of the* Cheerleaders

Janette Rallison

Walker & Company
New York

First published in the United States of America in 2007 by
Walker Publishing Company, Inc.
Distributed to the trade by Holtzbrinck Publishers

For information about permission to reproduce selections from
this book, write to Permissions, Walker & Company,
104 Fifth Avenue, New York, New York 10011

Library of Congress Cataloging-in-Publication Data
Rallison, Janette.
Revenge of the cheerleaders / by Janette Rallison.
p.   cm.
Summary: High school cheerleader Chelsea seeks revenge against her younger sister's rock-and-roller boyfriend after he embarrasses her once too often, but when she falls for his older brother, things become really complicated.
ISBN-13: 978-0-8027-8999-0 • ISBN-10: 0-8027-8999-4 (hardcover)
[1. Dating (Social customs)—Fiction. 2. High schools—Fiction.
3. Schools—Fiction. 4. Brothers and sisters—Fiction. 5. Cheerleading—Fiction.
6. Washington (State)—Fiction.] I. Title.
PZ7.R13455Re 2007   [Fic]—dc22   2007002372

Visit Walker & Company's Web site at www.walkeryoungreaders.com

Book design by Nicole Gastonguay
Typeset by Westchester Book Composition
Printed in the U.S.A. by Quebecor World Fairfield
2 4 6 8 10 9 7 5 3 1

All papers used by Walker & Company are natural, recyclable products made from wood grown in well-managed forests. The manufacturing processes conform to the environmental regulations of the country of origin.

To everyone out there who knows
that reading can and should be fun.
You're the people who make
writing worthwhile.

Special thanks to Devon Felsted for not only answering my
Pullman questions, but for even knowing how many
stoplights there are in town. I miss the small-town life!

Chapter 1

My wings and halo were too large. I looked more like a pale butterfly than an angel, but a person can't be picky when it comes to Halloween costumes, and it's not like I'd paid for it. My best friend, Samantha, dug it out of her old drama costumes for me.

I had spent the last hour transforming my long blonde hair into glittery curls, and now she used the curling iron to even up one of my ringlets. After she hairsprayed it into place, she took a step back from me. "You're gorgeous, Chelsea."

"You don't think the dress is too tight?"

She tilted her head. "Well, you don't want to look too much like an angel, do you?"

"Not if Mike and Naomi are going to be there." Mike is my ex-boyfriend and Naomi—newly crowned home-coming queen—is my ex-friend and the girl he dumped me for. This is why I have to look extra good whenever I go places where they might be. And because Pullman, Washington, is a small town, that's just about everywhere. Super-models probably slack off more with their looks than I have over the last month.

Mike and Naomi would almost certainly be at Rachel's masquerade party. It's a standing rule: when any of us on the cheerleading squad have a party, we invite the whole football team. Mike is a running back. So he was sure to come.

Samantha gave her long green medieval princess dress one last look in the mirror and fastened a rhinestone tiara atop her bun. I'd already told her that medieval princesses didn't actually wear tiaras, but Samantha just shrugged, and said, "Well, they should have."

You can't argue with that kind of logic.

Besides, the tiara worked for Samantha. She's the type of girl who looks likes she's destined to become a beauty pageant queen. Perhaps I wasn't destined to ever be an angel though, because I kept knocking my wings into things as I walked through her house.

"How am I going to drive in this?" I asked, trying not to scrape the pictures off the hallway wall as I passed by. It had taken ten minutes to pin them on the dress. I wasn't about to unpin them for the car ride.

"Maybe you could lean forward," Samantha suggested. "Or roll down the window and drive sideways. The police wouldn't dare pull over an angel. That has to be some sort of sin."

Before we walked out the front door, I caught a glimpse of my reflection in the window and paused to straighten out my halo. It was really just a headband with a wire sticking straight up and a metallic silver garland that circled over my head. Only all those years of being shoved in Samantha's closet had bent it into an odd oval shape and it kept tilting down. "Why don't I just catch a ride with you?" I hesitated mid-step. "Although, if Mike and Naomi are especially obnoxious I might want to leave early . . ."

Samantha fished her car keys out of a small sequined purse, which also hadn't been around in the middle ages, but you know, should have been. "Don't let them bother you so much. The best way to show Mike that you don't care is to date someone else. Remember, there are more fish in the sea, and better yet, more players on the football team."

We walked out into the cold night air, and I wished I'd found a warmer costume. Something that involved a coat and scarf. "I'm not dating anyone else from the football team," I said. "Cheerleaders shouldn't. It's too hard to cheer for guys who've dumped you. Lately I've been tempted to clap every time he's tackled—and see, the crowd might notice that."

Samantha opened her car door and slid inside. "So find someone else. Football players won't be the only guys at the party."

I didn't answer her. The rest of the girls on the cheerleading squad always bounced back from breakups as though they were nothing. As though "breakup" wasn't synonymous with rejection, failure, and a bunch of other painful words. I couldn't forget that Mike had seen me from the inside, had seen everything I was, and then decided he didn't want me.

When he broke up with me he told me—and these are his exact words—that he was sorry he'd been seeing Naomi behind my back, but she understood him better. He didn't even take responsibility for shredding my heart. It was all somehow my fault because I hadn't understood him.

Anyway, my ego still hadn't recovered; so I wasn't about to rush it into harm's way again.

I got into the car on the passenger side, and leaned over the dashboard so my wings wouldn't bend. There is no comfortable way to wear a seat belt while simultaneously contorting over the dashboard, which is probably why real angels fly everywhere.

When we pulled up to Rachel's house, we saw Mike, Naomi, and her sidekick Kyra, just stepping out of his car—proving that my timing is lousy. I had to wrestle the seat belt away from my wings, then turn and dip sideways to get out.

Mike wore doctor scrubs. Kyra had red spots painted on her face so she looked like a patient, and Naomi wore a skimpy nurse's outfit.

Yeah, right—she understood him better. Naomi probably doesn't understand the directions on a box of macaroni and cheese. This may be the reason she's so thin. It's hard to gain weight when you have to chew through the cardboard to get to your dinner.

Mike paused by our car as I extracted myself from the front seat. "Let me guess: you guys are Cinderella and her fairy godmother?"

"No," Samantha said with mock disgust. "If Chelsea was a fairy godmother she'd be hauling around a wand and a pumpkin."

Naomi sent me a forced smile. "Oh, you're a giant moth, right?"

See, this is why costume parties are a bad idea.

"No," I said, smoothing out my dress. "Moths don't wear halos."

Naomi's gaze went up to the silver garland encircling my head. "A halo? Is that what that is? I thought it was supposed to be a lightbulb. You know, because moths always fly into them."

Kyra lowered her voice and leaned toward Naomi. "Yeah, and Chelsea could use a few lightbulbs going off over her head."

Mike pretended not to hear this, but I knew he had. He shrugged and said, "See you guys later."

Not if I could help it.

Maybe it wouldn't have been as uncomfortable to be around him if things hadn't gotten ugly between Naomi and me beforehand. After he dumped me, Naomi came up to me during school and said she hoped we could still be friends.

Like I was going to be friends with the girl who had snuck around with my boyfriend behind my back. I just think not. Instead of making nice, I had told her exactly what I thought of her.

It was one of those hallway moments where everyone stops what they're doing to stare at you, then they look away quickly and pretend they have stuff to get out of their locker.

After that, our friends had to take sides. Naomi got Kyra and a small entourage of girls who tried too hard to be popular; I got my friends on the cheerleading squad.

I wish that were the end of it, but since then, Naomi and her friends have done their best to bad-mouth me to anybody and everybody at school. The term "white trash" has come out of her mouth on more than one occasion.

And okay, I'll be the first to admit that my house isn't the nicest one in town. Single mothers who work in nursing homes generally can't provide those. But I am not white trash. I know this because my father's side of the family is definitely white trash and I've met them. I can tell the difference.

Since our breakup, Mike goes out of his way to be extra nice to me. I guess it's guilt or something. I'd tell him to spare me the effort, but I sort of enjoy the way Naomi grits her teeth every time he talks to me. A few more months of this and she'll have nothing but tooth stubs left in her mouth.

My cell phone rang and I took it out of my purse, glad for the excuse to let Mike's group get ahead of us. It was my mom, her voice sounding breathless and worried.

"Do you know where Adrian is?"

Adrian is my fifteen-year-old sister who has delusions of being twenty-five. Sometimes she disappears and it usually means she is off with her boyfriend, Rick, trying in some way to ruin her life. Lately my mom is worried that she's started drinking. I'd like to think that Adrian just hints at going to those types of parties to drive Mom crazy, but I'm not sure.

Adrian used to swear she would never touch alcohol. We'd seen firsthand how it had messed up our dad's life. After you watch your father stumble into the walls on a daily basis, it just makes the Michelob life seem a lot less glamorous.

I pressed my cell phone to my ear. "Isn't she at Stefy's Halloween party?"

"I just talked to Stefy's mom. She hasn't seen Adrian at all. I called both Rick and Adrian's cell phones and neither picked up. Any idea where she could be?"

Before I'd left for Samantha's house, I'd seen Adrian in the bathroom applying a fake nose and chin to her face. She'd also bought a black wig, pointy hat, and green makeup to transform her into the Wicked Witch of the West.

"She must be at someone's costume party. There aren't a lot of places you can go and blend in when you're bright green."

"Could she be at your party?" Mom asked.

Doubtful. She didn't like to hang out with me or my friends. "I'll look and see," I said.

"Check around with Rick's friends," Mom said. "One of them might know where they are."

Rick is a senior like me, but that is as far as our similarities go. Rick has more body piercings than I have earrings, wears a wardrobe that looks like it was lifted off a homeless man, and keeps dying his hair random colors. Last week he and Adrian both dyed their hair maroon, which if you ask me is carrying the "couple" thing way too far.

"I'll ask around," I said.

"Let me know as soon as you find out anything," Mom said.

I hung up the phone and walked with Samantha into Rachel's house. I saw Rachel immediately; she sat among a circle of football players, looking like a perfect bronze goddess in a toga. We're not talking a bed sheet, we're talking an authentic-looking Roman dress that she probably used when she showed up as Venus in half the senior guys' dreams.

Right now Rachel was between boyfriends, but this was no doubt a situation that would be rectified by the end of the night. Rachel is never without a guy for long.

Aubrie, my other friend on the cheerleading squad, sat next to her in a gymnast outfit. This was technically almost not a costume, since Aubrie is one of those girls who came out of the womb completely able to land a backflip. We always give her the hardest parts in any cheerleading routine because she makes it look like gravity doesn't apply to her.

A few of the football players called out hellos to me, and I smiled and answered back, but the whole time I glanced around the room looking for anyone in a witch costume. I didn't see any of those, but I did locate Craig Van Dam, one of Rick's delinquent friends. He sat in a corner with some guys from the team, all of whom were oozing fake blood from various parts of their bodies.

Usually I steered clear of Rick and all things associated with him, but I strolled up to Craig while Samantha went over to talk to Rachel and Aubrie. "Hey, Craig, do you know where Rick is?"

Craig eyed my costume, but didn't comment on it. "Rick's band is playing at the CUB tonight. Some fund-raiser thing."

The CUB is short for Compton Union Building, a main hub on the Washington State University campus. Generally high school students didn't go there, but the other two guys in Rick's band graduated last year and were now freshman at WSU. So far I'd never known Rick's band—accurately named Rick and the Deadbeats—to play anywhere besides his garage, but I guess fund-raisers aren't choosy about the quality of music at their events.

"It's a costume affair?" I asked.

"Must be; Rick went as a vampire."

Adrian had to be there. Why she didn't just tell my mom in the first place that she was going—well, I knew why she hadn't. Since the dance was up on campus, my mom probably wouldn't have let her go. Mom says she's too young to hang out with college kids.

I thanked Craig, then walked down Rachel's hallway and called my mom. After I told her what I learned she was silent for a moment.

"Adrian might be there, but Stefy's mom said some of the girls had talked about going to a dance at Moscow High and a group of them left for that. I'm halfway there now. Will you check up on campus?"

"Mom, I just got to the party."

It was the wrong thing to say. My mom's voice came back across the line in a torrent of emotion. "This isn't exactly how I planned on spending my evening either. I have six bags of candy sitting by our door and no one to give it out. Now I'm going to be known as the neighbor who stiffed all the little kids on Halloween. I have to chase around heaven knows where looking for Adrian—and all because she can't follow simple rules, like letting me know where she is, and not running off without permission, and answering her stupid cell phone. Why am I paying the bill for it if she won't even pick up?" In the time it took for her to draw in a breath,

Mom's voice changed from anger to a near sob. "So I'm sorry to interrupt your party, but I think finding your sister is more important."

"Okay, Mom, I'll check on campus."

She let out a breath, composing herself. "Thanks, Chelsea. I'm glad I can count on you, at least."

Sometimes being the responsible daughter is the pits.

Chapter 2

I'd already hung up before I remembered that I'd left my car at Samantha's house. I trudged off to ask her to take me back to her home. She was busy text messaging Logan, her boyfriend, asking if he could get off work early to come to the party. They'd been going out since last spring and were still in that giddy-in-love-can't-be-separated-from-you stage. The rest of us simultaneously endured and envied the way Samantha floated around in his presence.

Apparently the news from Logan wasn't good, because when I explained the situation, she said she'd drive up to campus with me. "Two pairs of eyes are better than one and besides, you still can't drive with those wings."

I knew she didn't really want to come. She was just being nice about it. All the way up to campus she chatted happily with me like it was a normal thing for us to spend Halloween night trying to track down my missing sister.

Part of me worried that something bad might have happened to Adrian. A section of my stomach balled itself into a knot and wouldn't be reassured no matter how many times

I told it that Adrian hadn't been abducted, she was just being her usual thoughtless self.

The farther we drove, the madder I got at her for doing this to Mom and me. I mean, Adrian didn't care how many knots she tied in my stomach or the fact that Mom was near tears or that our house would probably be egged by angry trick-or-treaters. Adrian didn't care as long as she got to do what she wanted to do. By the time Samantha and I had parked and walked to the CUB, I was ready to grab Adrian by her witch wig and yell, "Forget Dorothy, you better worry about me dropping a house on you."

We walked inside the building and followed the noise up the stairs. Yep, it was Rick's band all right. I recognized the tune. Rick had given Adrian a CD of his songs, so I am frequently forced to listen to them vibrating through her bedroom wall.

We walked toward a table that stood by the door to the ballroom. A girl and two guys—respectively, Little Bo Peep, a wizard, and Clark Kent—sat in front of a money box.

Great. I hadn't taken into account that I needed money to get into this and I didn't have any. I glanced at Samantha. "Do you have cash on you?"

"Just a couple of dollars and some spare change."

I walked up to the table anyway, keeping my eyes on Clark Kent. Which wasn't hard to do because, hey, the guy looked like Clark Kent. His white-collared shirt was half open to reveal a blue T-shirt with a large red S printed on it, and judging from the guy's build, it was truth in advertising.

I smiled at him. "Hi, um, have you seen any witches lately?"

"Does my chemistry teacher count?" He flashed a set of perfect teeth that made him look even more attractive. I nearly had to steady myself against the table.

"No, actually I'm thinking younger and greener."

Clark Kent considered this for a moment. "I guess we've had a few of the broom-stick persuasion come by tonight."

"Could we go inside and check?" Samantha asked. "We're just looking for a friend."

Bo Peep's expression stiffened. "It costs five dollars to get in."

"But we're not here to dance," I said.

"Pity," Clark Kent said, and for a couple of seconds I forgot about Adrian, forgot that I had to get in, and smiled at him again.

"If they just want to look around—" the wizard started, but Bo Peep cut him off.

"It still costs five dollars. We already said no exceptions."

Clark Kent shrugged an apology in our direction. "We're raising money for the homeless."

"What luck," I said. "Because I happen to be homeless. Instead of sending me money, can you just let me go inside and—"

"No," Bo Peep said, and glared at me. This is what happens, I suppose, to people who tend sheep all day. They lose their sense of humor.

Still, I was not about to give up. "We would be happy to pay you," I said with a sigh, "but angels don't use money and medieval princesses always barter with land. The best we can

13

do is to bestow a few blessings or give you some prime real estate in the parking lot."

Clark Kent laughed. His eyes turned warm and they struck me as familiar somehow. I'd seen those eyes before. Where? I stared at him trying to figure it out, which probably wasn't polite, but he didn't seem to mind. He stared back at me with a grin.

Samantha held out a hand imploringly. "It would really only take a few minutes, and we have a couple of dollars. Could two dollars buy us a few minutes?"

Samantha opened her purse, but Bo Peep shook her head so that her store-bought curls bounced angrily around her head. "It's five dollars. No matter how long you go in."

I really had the urge to tell her to go look for some sheep, preferably off a steep cliff, but I didn't.

Clark Kent leaned forward and pulled his wallet from his back pocket. Before I realized what he was doing, he took a ten-dollar bill and handed it to me. My fingers tingled from where he touched them.

"I want a blessing for this," he said, looking at me intently.

"What kind?" I asked.

"I want to dance with an angel."

For the second time that night I completely forgot about my sister. "I think I could arrange that."

A grin stretched across his face. "Good. After you find your friend let me know."

Oh yeah, Adrian.

I handed the money to Bo Peep. "Do we need our hands stamped or something?"

She picked up a stamp from the table and pounded orange pumpkins onto our wrists. "All right, go in." You could tell it hurt her to say the words. We'd only walked a few feet away when I heard her turn to Clark Kent and say, "You're such a sucker for a pretty face."

"Hey, helping damsels in distress is my job," he said.

We walked into the ballroom, and it took a few moments for my eyes to adjust to the dark. Rick stood on a platform, decked out as Dracula and grabbing his electric guitar with such force that it looked like he was trying to wind the thing up. One of his band-mates sat behind a set of drums, the other stood off to the side with a bass guitar.

Where was Adrian? She had to be close by; somewhere in the Rick adoration zone. I didn't walk through the dance floor, I couldn't maneuver around people with my wings, so we walked around the circumference of the room, looking. In the darkness, sports figures, monsters, genies, and more cats than you could count—probably because WSU's mascot is the cougar—all moved to the music. I spotted a witch, but it was just a freckle-faced coed who wore a pointy hat, not Adrian.

I saw one man without a costume and he looked so out of place that I stared at him for several seconds before I realized he was a security guard. He stood in the back of the room, arms folded and looking bored.

I made my way up to the front of the room. Samantha followed but we didn't talk. The music didn't allow for it.

I suppose it was too much to hope that Rick wouldn't notice me. After all, it's pretty hard to overlook a girl towing mammoth-sized wings on her back.

Between songs Rick went to the mike and said, "Hey, great costumes, everybody. I especially like yours, Chels, because what says Halloween better than a giant anemic butterfly?"

I ignored him and kept looking around for Adrian.

"Anybody got a jumbo-sized can of Raid?" he called.

Some people shouldn't be allowed access to microphones. Especially people who don't like me. A few people in the crowd stared at me and chuckled.

Rick leaned in closer to the mike and added, "Why aren't there ever any six-foot tarantulas around when you need them?"

This pretty much sums up my relationship with Rick. It's been this way since last year, when Rick and Samantha both ran for school president. He was a jerk during the campaign, and by the time the election was over, we hated each other. Which makes the fact that my little sister dates him that much more annoying.

I moved away from the front of the room. Adrian wouldn't be up by the stage anymore—not after Rick had drawn attention to me. Now that she knew I was here, she'd be hightailing it to somewhere less visible. Where? Deep in the crowd? The bathrooms, maybe?

Then I saw her. I recognized the hat, wig, and green makeup. She strolled toward the refreshment table in an unconcerned manner.

So maybe she hadn't been paying attention while Rick asked for volunteers with insecticide—either that, or she didn't care that I'd come after her. I quickened my step and followed after her.

"Adrian!"

She didn't turn around. She either didn't hear me because of the music or she ignored me. Probably the latter.

I gritted my teeth together and went faster. "Adrian!" I shouted.

Now she and several other people glanced over their shoulders at me. I have to admit, she'd done a good job with her makeup. Her putty nose curved down and her chin pointed up so that they almost met. Several warts grew on her face and she'd done something to her cheekbones so that they looked exaggerated. If I hadn't been with her when she bought the costume, I wouldn't have recognized her.

Without answering me, Adrian turned back around and went on.

"Don't you dare walk away from me," I said and pushed my pace. "You know you're not supposed to be here."

She glanced over her shoulder again, looked at me nervously, then walked faster.

Samantha trotted up to my side. "Do you want me to talk with her? Maybe if we call your mom and tell her we'll stay here and chaperone Adrian—"

"No," I said. "Adrian has to learn that she can't treat people this way. She can't just worry us, and make us run all over town looking for her, and pretend it doesn't matter." I turned away from Samantha and watched Adrian's retreating back. "Hey," I yelled again. "You had better turn around and come with me right now."

She glanced back at me again with wide eyes, but instead of stopping and waiting for me, she took off in a sprint.

Without a word I hiked up my dress and ran after her. "Don't think you can get away from me!" I yelled. I knew I could catch her. I've always been faster. True, I wore white ballet slippers which had roughly the same traction as cotton balls, but my determination gave me extra speed.

Adrian ran to the refreshment table, then made a sharp left. I followed. Okay, actually I bumped into the table, and as I turned to go after her, my wings knocked over a large stack of paper plates and several cookies. They fell to the ground and scattered in my wake as I hurried after Adrian.

I heard someone from behind the table yell, "Hey!" and I called out, "Sorry!" but didn't slow down. A few moments later I had gained on my sister again. Her black cape fluttered out behind her, almost within my grasp.

"You are so dead!" I called out.

"Leave me alone!" she called back. At least I think that's what she said, because Rick crescendoed into a loud part of the song just then and it muffled everything out.

She ran behind the platform that the band stood on. It was darker back here and a bunch of cables for the electrical equipment snaked from the platform to the wall. I slowed my pace so I didn't trip on them. Adrian didn't and managed to snag one of them with her foot. I know this because suddenly both the electric guitar and Rick's voice stopped booming across the room.

An overall improvement, really.

I didn't have time to stop and plug it back in. Adrian dashed out a side door and I turned and followed her into the hallway. Well, technically I slid into a bunch of people who stood by the doorway chatting, but after that I followed.

Stumbling out into the hallway, I struggled to regain my balance, then set out after Adrian again. As Adrian weaved in between groups of people, Samantha ran up beside me and called out to her, "We just need to talk to you!"

Adrian didn't slow down and I was losing patience and ground. My wings kept knocking into people, which jostled me back and forth in the hallway like a pinball. "Just grab her!" I told Samantha.

And so she did. She dashed forward to close the gap, and grabbed hold of her arm. Adrian tried to jerk away, which pulled Samantha into her. They fell to the ground in a heap.

Samantha's tiara rolled across the floor and Adrian's witch hat and wig flipped off.

And that's when I noticed the witch wasn't Adrian.

Adrian had dyed her hair maroon. This person was brunette.

Oops.

"I've got her," Samantha called to me, as she sat up.

The witch tried to pull away from Samantha again, and screamed, "Help! Get away from me!"

Samantha turned at the sound of the girl's voice—which, now that we were away from the noise, didn't sound at all like Adrian's. Samantha dropped her hands off the girl, and let out a scream herself.

I walked over to them. My mouth moved, but for several moments no words came out. Then they all rushed out at once. "I'm so sorry. Really, I just—I thought you were some-one else. Another Wicked Witch of the West. She looks just like you. Well, in the dark from the back, anyway." I picked up her wig and hat from the floor and handed them to her. "You know, one day this will all seem funny."

She glared as she took her things from me.

"Maybe not today," I added. "But one day."

I didn't have time to say anything else because the secu-rity guard pushed his way through the crowd of people and yelled, "What's going on here?"

The witch pulled herself up off the floor and pointed a finger in my direction. "I was minding my own business when that psycho-butterfly girl started yelling at me, and when I tried to get away from her, she chased me out here and told that other girl to tackle me."

The guard turned and stared at me. My mouth went dry. "It was all a mistake," I said. "I thought she was my little sister." No one moved. No one spoke. "Great makeup job," I added.

The witch let out a humph and said, "And you didn't re-alize I wasn't your sister when I yelled out, 'Leave me alone' and ran away from you?"

I shrugged apologetically. "It's something she might do."

The girl arranged her wig and hat back onto her head. "Well, we don't have to wonder why, do we?"

"I'm really sorry," I said again.

The guard looked between Samantha and me, then growled, "You two, come with me."

We did. And this time I managed to follow without run-ning into things. He marched us down the hall, away from the ballroom, lecturing us about our rowdy behavior. It was people like us, he said, that ruined things for everybody else. What if the administration decided not to let the students put on more fund-raisers because a few people didn't have the decency to behave in public? Had we thought of *that* before we'd gone careening into the refreshment table and jumping on innocent people?

Well, obviously not, but I didn't say so.

He kept lecturing us, and our only saving grace was that he'd taken us away from the crowd. I don't think I could have stood to be chewed out in front of Rick or the Clark Kent guy.

The Clark Kent guy. The thought of him made my shoulders droop. He'd paid for me to get in, and I'd told him I'd dance with him. Now he'd think I'd just used him for his money and disappeared.

The guard led us to an exit, opened the door for us, and said he'd better not see us anywhere near the dance again. The next moment we were outside in the cold night air.

We walked side by side toward the car, moving quickly. "I'm sorry," I told Samantha, "but how was I to know? It was the exact same costume that Adrian bought."

Samantha spoke in a low voice, "Don't tell anyone about this night. Not Rachel. Not Aubrie. It's a secret we carry to our graves. Even if Rick hears about it, we deny everything. It was another medieval princess and angel who got tossed out of the dance, not us."

"Right," I said, and really hoped Rick hadn't been paying attention as I rammed the refreshment table while chasing a hapless stranger. I mean, once that story got around, Naomi would never let go of it.

On the way home my mom called my cell phone. "Guess what? Stefy's mom just phoned and it turns out Adrian has been there the entire time. Stefy's mom just didn't recognize her because she looked so different in her witch costume." My mom let out a relieved chuckle. "So I'm sorry I made you leave your party, but you have to admit, it's funny."

Maybe one day, but not today.

Chapter 3

On Monday at school I waited for Rick or one of his friends to say something obnoxious to me in the hallway, like: "Hey—tackle any more strangers lately?" Or "This is just a guess, but you flunked out of guardian angel class, didn't you?"

No one said anything out of the ordinary though, which must mean he didn't know. This was the first good news I'd had in a long time.

After school we had an extra cheerleading practice at my house. Extra because we had a pep assembly the next day and we wanted to make sure we had our routine down. Our cheerleading advisor, Mrs. Jones, had gone to a cheerleading conference and come back with a great choreography to "Be True to Your School" but it was more difficult than the routines we usually did.

Forty-five minutes into practice—and still without us doing the whole thing perfectly—Samantha walked to the CD player and pushed the off button. "We need to take a break."

I started to protest, but Aubrie and Rachel headed to my

kitchen, moving very quickly for people who were agreeing that they needed a rest.

I went with them, and while I poured everyone drinks, Samantha said, "I think we've almost got it. One more time through is all we need."

Rachel eyed Samantha's still-in-place long blonde hair and perfectly applied makeup. "You just want to end early so you can go hang out with your boyfriend."

Samantha gave her a satisfied smile. "Right."

She had totally missed the point. Love apparently makes you immune to sarcasm.

"I think we need to go through it until—" I took a sip of my drink, "we do it flawlessly a bunch of times."

This brought forth groans from Aubrie and Rachel. "It's a pep assembly," Aubrie said, "not the Olympics."

"I can't mess up in front of Naomi and her minions."

Rachel let out a sigh. "Since Mike broke up with you, you've become an absolute perfectionist." She turned to Samantha and Aubrie as though I wasn't in the room. "You know, we'd all have a lot more free time if Chelsea got a boyfriend. We should do something about that."

"Maybe we could take up a collection to buy her one," Aubrie said.

"Or we could set her by the road with a sign that says, 'Will cheer for hot guy,'" Samantha added.

Rachel sighed into her drink. "I know I'd cheer for a hot guy."

Right. Poor her. Apparently she hadn't found Mr. Right at her party.

While I finished my drink, Adrian and Rick strolled into the kitchen. Adrian had taken to gelling and hairspraying her short hair so that it stuck up in random angles, resembling a maroon feather duster. Today Rick's hair was almost as messy.

Adrian went to the cupboard, grabbed a bag of Cheetos, and sat down at the table with them. She used to hate Cheetos. We used to laugh at anyone who ate food with so much orange powder on it that you could use it to write messages on the table. But Rick liked them and that changed everything.

He pushed past me and stood in front of the fridge. "Well, if it isn't the cheerleading quadruplets: Blonde, Blonder, Blondest"—he nodded in my direction—"and Dangerously Blonde. Are you done jumping around in the living room, or is it still unsafe for normal people to come out?"

Rachel folded her arms and eyed his shirt, which looked like it had been spray painted by thugs and then thrown under a moving truck. "Since when are you a normal person?"

He let out a snort. "Like you'd know the difference."

It was one thing for Rick to insult *me* at my house—which trust me, he did often enough—but it was another thing for him to insult my friends at my house. Instead of ignoring him, and saying my usual prayer that Adrian would wake up from her almost trancelike adoration of the guy, I turned to him and said, "Do you need something? I mean, besides the obvious fashion lesson?"

He sneered at me, reached into the fridge, and grabbed the last two cans of soda. "Sorry to take it all," he said, "but hey, it's probably for the best. If you keep dipping into the treats, it won't take long before you can put a lot more besides the word 'Cheer' on your rear end." He threw one can to Adrian, then eyed me over with a smile. "Looks like you're almost to sentence length as we speak."

First of all, I am in no danger of being able to spell out sentences on my shorts. And while I'm bringing up the inaccuracy of Rick's insults, I'll also mention that only three of us on the cheerleading squad are blonde. Rachel has brown hair that she highlights. Rick just says anything that he thinks will bother us.

I walked away from Rick and back to where Adrian sat flipping Cheetos into her mouth. In a low voice I said, "You know you're not supposed to have boys over when Mom isn't home."

Adrian rolled her eyes. "Yeah, and have I thanked you lately for that rule?"

I did not make that rule. I've often wished I had the power to make rules at our house because there are a lot of things I'd change, and most of them have to do with Adrian. For example, right after I made our property a Rick-free zone, I would restrict the amount of dreary clothing Adrian wears. I mean, sure, I like a little black dress as well as the next woman, and black pants are versatile—but Adrian wears all black, every day. It's like living in a funeral home. And the friends she brings home usually smell so badly of cigarette smoke that you have to ventilate the place after they leave. Seriously, one day she'll bring over too many and they'll set off the smoke alarm.

I didn't make the rule about Rick not being allowed over when Mom wasn't home. Mom asked me questions about him and then made the rule all by herself.

I put down my drink. "Come on guys, let's run through our routine one more time."

My friends didn't argue the point. Probably because they didn't want to stay with Rick and Adrian any more than I did. We went back to the living room, turned up the song loud enough to drown out any conversation in the kitchen, and did the number perfectly. In sync. In step. And in time.

"We're ready," Samantha said as the music ended.

Rachel held her hair off her shoulders. "Which is a good thing because I'm totally sick of that song."

From the kitchen doorway, where they had been watching us, Rick called, "Finally something we have in common. Tell Chelsea to get some taste in music."

"And I was just about to give you the same advice," I called back.

Adrian flopped down on the couch, put her feet on the wall and leaned back so that her head nearly touched the floor. She looked at me from her upside-down perch. "You know, you should start being nice to Rick. One day he'll be famous."

"Uh huh." That was all her comment merited in the way of a rebuttal. According to Adrian, Rick is the next Elvis. Well, Elvis in a grungy Goth sort of way. It wouldn't hurt her to live in this fantasy world, or at least it wouldn't hurt me, but lately she and Rick had reached insufferable ego levels, thanks to a new show, *High School Idol*.

The makers of *High School Idol* billed it as *American Idol* for teens, and were unfortunately doing an audition in our town. This was about the most exciting thing Pullman had seen since, well, since ever, really. It didn't matter that auditions were also taking place in L.A., New York, Chicago, Miami, and Dallas, or that the winner would certainly come from one of the big cities. The producers wanted a contestant from rural America to show that the next superstar could come from anywhere. So as an oddity, a ratings-getter, they were offering a slot to one teenage singer or group from Pullman.

I figured they were stopping here mostly to make fun of us. I mean, really, how could a town that only had about seven hundred kids in high school ever compete with L.A.? They just figured we were a bunch of hicks who'd dress in gingham and sing off-key to *Sound of Music* songs.

Only no one saw it that way besides me. It's all anyone talked about at school. One of us would be on TV performing in front of the nation. What if one of us won the whole contest? People who didn't know clef notes from Cliffs Notes were suddenly breaking out into song in the middle of the school hallways. It was like being trapped in some bad musical.

I can sing, but I'm a little too realistic to think I'll suddenly be discovered and dropped into a limo on its way to Epic Records headquarters. My friends and I aren't even auditioning. What's the point?

But Adrian and Rick are convinced that fate designed this show just to launch Rick into stardom. And I've had to hear about it since they announced the auditions a week ago. Fortunately only three weeks are left until they come and we can put this whole unfortunate episode behind us. I probably won't rub it in too badly when Rick is rejected.

My friends picked up their pom-poms and backpacks and made their way to the door. They probably would have stayed longer—well, at least Rachel and Aubrie would have—if Rick hadn't been there harassing us.

As Aubrie left, she cast a glance in Rick's direction and then looked back at me. "You can come over to my house for dinner if you want."

Aubrie is an angel. I didn't even hesitate. I walked out the door and called over my shoulder, "I'm going to Aubrie's. Tell Mom when she gets home."

I knew Adrian probably wouldn't, but that didn't worry me. Mom can reach me by cell phone. Besides, she doesn't hassle me much about where I go. This is the one advantage to having a rebellious little sister. In comparison, you're always the good child.

ఎ ఎ ఎ

When I came home, I could hear Adrian and Mom in the kitchen fighting. Mom went on about trust, and how Adrian needed to obey the rules; then Adrian went on about how Mom was never home so the rule wasn't fair. Mom said something, I couldn't hear what, but Adrian stomped off to her room with the declaration that she hated us all.

If I shut my eyes, I can still see Adrian in pigtails following me around with puppy like adoration, but not long ago she shook off her affection for me, like a person shakes rain off an umbrella.

After Adrian had slammed her bedroom door shut, Mom

came into the living room to grill me for information. *How long had Rick been over?* I didn't know because I left shortly after he called me Dangerously Blonde. *Why had he come over?* Probably just to torment me. *What had Adrian and he done when he was over?* Insult me, my friends, my music, and drink the rest of the soda.

Then Mom laid into me for leaving the two of them alone together. She went on about how I should have stuck around to be their chaperone because Adrian was almost sixteen—she was old enough to seriously mess up her life by doing something stupid with Rick.

"You know your sister doesn't have any sense," Mom said. "If she had her way, Rick would be moving in here, and you'd have to introduce him to your friends as 'my brother-in-law'."

Chilling, yes, but probably true. Still, I didn't see what I could do about it. It's not like Adrian listened to me anymore. After the election fiasco, I'd told her she ought to dump Rick, and then I'd spent the entire summer trying to set her up with all sorts of guys just to pry her away from his clutches.

Most little sisters would appreciate this, considering that the guys I know are way cooler than the people she hangs out with. But no, it only made her more devoted to Rick because, "He isn't like other guys."

Exactly. Other guys are better.

I tried to explain all of this to Mom, but the more I did, the more Mom insisted that I needed to watch Adrian.

"Bad boys have a certain attraction, but they grow up to be bad men, and we all know where that leads." She meant my father. He was the type of fate we had to keep Adrian from. Because really, the only nice thing you can say about my father is that he stays far away from us. My parents divorced when I was eight and now he lives in Chicago in some low-rent dive he shares with several colonies of cockroaches.

Still, I didn't think me keeping an eye on Adrian was going to do any good. She didn't need an eye. She needed an ankle bracelet and a prison guard.

Chapter 4

I wore my cheerleading uniform to school the next day. We wear them on game days as a reminder for the students to come see the game. I always feel on display when I wear it. Somehow it transforms me from Chelsea the normal person into someone who's upbeat and peppy. You're not supposed to be depressed while wearing a cheerleading uniform. You can't have a bad hair day or skimp on your makeup. It's like going to school as Barbie. Anyway, I didn't really feel like smiling and being full of school spirit, because as soon as I got to school I ran into Mike and Naomi strolling down the hallway holding hands.

He never held hands with me in school. They passed by me in a wave of coolness, and I walked on, feeling alone and acutely aware that the only guy who'd spoken to me today was Samantha's boyfriend, Logan. And all he'd said was, "Hey Chelsea, where's Samantha?"

Logan is so smitten with her that my hair could catch on fire and he wouldn't notice.

I could have gone and flirted with some of the football players to show Mike that I didn't care about him anymore.

That's what any other girl would have done. But I didn't feel like it. A lot of the guys on the team had known Mike was seeing Naomi behind my back and covered for him so I wouldn't find out.

How could I trust any of them after that?

Lately when I cheered and yelled, "Go team!" I mentally added where I wanted them to go.

So anyway, I didn't feel all that peppy come pep assembly time, but luckily Samantha was in charge of calling people down from the bleachers to participate in the games we'd set up. I just had to stand there, clap, and concentrate on not looking at the spot where Mike and Naomi sat. Then came our dance number to "Be True to Your School." It was the last thing we had planned for the assembly, the thing that was supposed to infuse the crowd with school spirit.

We stood in formation out on the gym floor. I told myself not to be nervous, even though the whole school sat in front of me watching. I would not trip. I would not accidentally fling one of my pom-poms into the crowd. We'd practiced this so many times that as soon as the music started, the dance moves would come to me automatically.

One of the J.V. cheerleaders stood by my boom box, waiting for Samantha's signal to start the music. Samantha walked to the microphone and smiled up at the audience. "This is a song that tells how we all feel about our school. If you know the words, sing along, and let's show the team how we feel about Greyhound pride." She walked back to our formation, then nodded to the J.V. cheerleader.

I clung to my pom-poms, already hearing the first few

beats of the song in my mind. But they didn't come. What blared into the gym wasn't a Beach Boys tune at all. It took me a few moments to react, to understand, and by then the crowd was already hooting and clapping. Instead of my Beach Boys CD, one of Rick's CDs was in my boom box.

In between the howling of the electric guitar, Rick's voice sang out, "School is a waste of time! School work corrodes your mind! Who needs teachers any more? Show 'em what trash bins are for."

All that came out before the J.V. cheerleader realized that this wasn't the song we had meant to play, and she needed to shut off the music.

Amid the noise from the crowd, everyone in the squad turned to me. "Where did that come from?" Samantha asked.

"What happened to our CD?" Rachel said at the same time.

Aubrie ran over to the boom box, I guess to check and make sure that our Beach Boys song wasn't somewhere hidden in it.

I felt my face flush. "I don't know. I never took our CD out of my boom box last night so I didn't bother to check to see if it was still there . . . Rick must have switched them after I left."

From the bleachers some of Rick's friends sang out the words to his song. Several teachers hurried over to stop them but that didn't keep the audience from joining in. After all, we had told people to sing along. Across the gym at the boom box, Aubrie held up Rick's CD and talked with Mrs. Jones, who kept shaking her head angrily. Then she strode over to us. "Well, it looks like you'll have to do the dance without the music."

We all glanced at one another. None of us wanted to stand in front of the school and do a dance number without music. It would be like synchronized miming or something.

"We won't be able to keep track of the beats without the music," I said. "We'll get out of synch and it will look strange. Let's just perform the number next pep assembly."

Mrs. Jones's voice came out in a clipped rhythm. "Tonight at the game our team will have to improvise when things get tough. Do you want to show them and the entire school that you're not willing to do the same?" She waved us back to our positions. "If you can't do the number without music, I'll go to the microphone and sing it for you."

"But . . ." I said, then looked at Samantha for help because I was too surprised to think of anything else to say.

Samantha said, "We don't mind waiting. It'll be better with the real music."

Mrs. Jones put her hands on her hips. "We are not ending this pep assembly by broadcasting a song about how school corrodes the mind." She waved a hand as though to wipe away any more protests. "It will be fine. I know the song by heart."

What could we say to that? We walked to our places in stunned silence—well, silence except for the crowd, who hooted and clapped when they saw us retake our positions. Crowds can sense when humiliation is about to happen.

Mrs. Jones walked to the microphone and took it in her hand. "I want you all to join me in singing, 'Be True to Your School.' It's for our team." Then she started singing.

No one joined her. I'm not sure whether it was because they didn't know the words (probably) or whether they just had more sense (also probably).

I'd like to say that Mrs. Jones is a great singer, but that would be lying. She sang the first few lines off-key and from there plunged into what could only be described as a rendition of the Beach Boys being pummeled by waves.

The only advantage to doing a dance number while your advisor butchers a song, is that everyone is so focused on her, they don't pay much attention to what you're doing. Rachel kept lagging behind the rest of us, I assume because she'd gone into shock or something, but I don't think anyone noticed. Then halfway through the first chorus Mrs. Jones stopped, then repeated the line she'd already sung—this is certain to throw off dancers, and half of us repeated the move that went with that line while the other half went on to the next move.

Which goes to show you that even when you don't think things can get worse, they really can.

She stumbled over a few more lines, repeated another one, and then stopped. It was clear she'd forgotten the words. It wasn't clear what we were supposed to do about it. After that "You have to improvise when things get tough" lecture I didn't expect her to quit, but I was a little afraid she'd start on another song altogether, and then we'd have to, I don't know, improvise Rockettes-style leg kicks in the background just for something to do while she sang.

Without thinking long enough to talk myself out of it, I jogged up to the microphone and stood by Mrs. Jones. She may have forgotten the lyrics, but I hadn't. I sang out and my voice stayed surprisingly steady. Mrs. Jones stopped singing all together and let me do a solo. Thank goodness I'd taken choir for three years. My voice never cracked.

A verse and a chorus later it was done. Everyone clapped, although this may have been because they were glad the whole thing was over.

I walked back to the group and it hit me, really hit me, that I'd just sung an a cappella solo in front of the whole school—friends, enemies, and ex-boyfriends alike. I'd probably be called Beach Girl for the rest of my senior year.

I was so going to kill Rick and Adrian for this.

ഇ ഇ ഇ

After the assembly the principal called the cheerleading squad into her office. We stood in a line—like soldiers in miniskirts—while she lectured us about playing anti-school music in a school-sponsored pep assembly. She asked us if "Show 'em what trash bins are for," was some sort of threat against the teachers and then quoted, word for word, the nonviolence policy the school had. She kept saying that the school took threats against people very seriously. I tried to explain that it had all been a mix-up, but she listened to my explanation with her lips pressed together in an angry frown, like she didn't believe me.

Talk about no sense of humor. The rest of the school was laughing about the incident, but no, not the principal.

Then she hauled Rick into the office to ask him about everything. Any other guy would have just fessed up that he and Adrian used my boom box to play his music, and they forgot to put my Beach Boys CD back, but not Rick. He was all, "I don't know why Chelsea played my song at the pep assembly. I never thought she was a fan of my music, but it looks like her taste in bands is improving." Then he gave me the thumbs-up sign. "Rock on, Chels."

Which made me think it hadn't been accidental at all. While the principal wrapped up her lecture with a stern warning that as cheerleaders we were ambassadors of the school and nothing like this had better happen again, I went over all the facts in my mind. We had a stereo system in the living room that had better speakers than my boom box. If the maroon-haired duo had wanted to listen to one of Rick's CDs, why had they chosen my boom box? Also, Adrian had a boom box in her room, why not use that one? And why lie about it to the principal?

The only reason I could see was that Rick wanted to make a fool of me at the pep assembly and now he wanted to get me in trouble.

As we all left the principal's office he turned back to me and said, "Hey, sorry this happened. I know how annoying it is when you're in front of a crowd, trying to perform and the music just disappears. Like say, when someone unplugs your band equipment in the middle of a concert."

"I didn't do that," I said. Which was technically true. I hadn't done it; the stranger I was chasing down had.

"Right. We're both innocent. And by the way, I'm innocent of anything else that happens too." He walked off before

I could respond. Which was probably for the best. I mean, there is a big difference between accidentally unplugging someone's equipment as you run by, and purposely setting out to sabotage, humiliate, and then get a whole squad of cheerleaders in trouble. Rachel and Aubrie hadn't even been at his dance. So why take revenge on them?

And what exactly did he mean that he was innocent of anything else that happened? Was that some sort of threat?

At lunch Samantha and I explained to Aubrie and Rachel what had happened at the dance. I pushed my salad around my plate without eating it. "So not only is he dating Adrian, now apparently he's trying to ruin my life, one painful day at a time."

Samantha pulled an apple from her lunch sack. "But you sounded really good up there singing."

"Did I?"

Aubrie nodded. "I wish I could sing that well."

My frustration with Rick momentarily evaporated while I considered this. I'd taken choir up until junior year, but to tell you the truth, I'd only signed up for it to get out of taking orchestra. I'd seen those flute and clarinet players wiping the spit out of their instruments and I'm sorry, but anything that involves large quantities of spit doesn't appeal to me. Mr. Metzerol, the music teacher, had never really forgiven me for not joining the show choir, but cheerleading practice was more important.

Still, it was nice to know that I hadn't made a total fool of myself. So there, Rick.

Rachel took a sip of her milk, considering. "I don't think his song had anything to do with getting back at you. I think he just wanted to advertise his party."

"What party?" I asked.

My friends exchanged glances. Rachel leaned toward me. "You haven't heard? Rick's band is playing at the Hilltop Friday night. He rented out the place for his party. He's practically invited the entire senior class."

"His friends are passing out flyers about it," Aubrie said. "Adrian gave me one."

Now that she mentioned it, I had seen people carrying around pieces of blue paper, but I hadn't asked anyone what they were, and everybody who talked to me in classes were too busy commenting on my assembly performance (Hey, when does the music video come out?) to mention anything else.

Aubrie took the flyer from her notebook and handed it to me. It showed a photocopied picture of Rick and two other guys standing with electric guitars. Blue Rick, by the way, looked about as normal as the real Rick. The flyer read, "Come dance today to tomorrow's hottest band: Rick and the Deadbeats!"

"They're moving out all the tables for the night and turning the restaurant into a dance floor," Rachel said. "Everyone is talking about it."

"Everyone is going," Aubrie added.

I put my fork down on my lunch tray. "To Rick's party? How did this happen? Since when did he become cool?"

Rachel stirred her spaghetti around with her fork. "Since he made you and Mrs. Jones sing a duet in front of the whole school and the rest of the cheerleading squad dance to it." She gave a small grunt. "Like I'm not going to have recurring nightmares about this day for the rest of my life."

Samantha patted my hand. "Don't listen to her. No one is laughing at us." More patting. "They're laughing with us. Really hard."

Rachel picked up her fork and waved it in Samantha's direction. "This is mostly your fault, you know."

"My fault?" she asked.

"Yeah, during elections last year when Rick was a royal jerk to you, you didn't do anything to put him back in his place. Remember how you were all about taking the high road? Well, apparently the high road leads straight to musical numbers with the P.E. teacher. Now Rick thinks he can do anything to us and get away with it."

Samantha thought about this, shaking her head. "Revenge doesn't solve anything. It just makes things worse."

Rachel let out an exasperated sigh. "That depends on who's doing the revenge and who's dancing to one of Mrs. Jones's solos in front of the whole school, doesn't it?"

And then Samantha cracked a smile. "If you can think of a way to get Rick dancing to Mrs. Jones in front of the whole school, I'll consider it. Until then, I say we just let the whole thing blow over. Let Rick have his party. So what if people are starting to think of him as some kind of rock star. I've heard Rick's music and no one will be that impressed with his band once they're trapped in a room with them. Just ignore him."

Easier said than done. I live in a home that's frequently

invaded by Rick. Still, I did think it would blow over. I thought his party and his attempts to get back at us wouldn't amount to anything. Which shows you that "psychic" wouldn't be a good career choice for me.

Chapter 5

I had no plans to go to Rick's party. I'm forced to see Rick more than I want, so why would I ever willingly go to a place he's performing?

My mom had other ideas. Apparently *going-to-Rick's-party* fell under the category of *chaperoning-my-sister*, which she wanted me to do. She was convinced alcohol would turn up at the party and she wanted to make sure I could yank Adrian home as soon as it appeared.

After my mom informed me of my chaperoning duties, I called Samantha. "Hi Sam, remember how you like Rick and want to give him another chance and all that?"

"I never said that," she said.

"Well, close enough, and I need someone to go to his party with me. What are you doing Friday night?"

There was a pause and then, "Wait a minute, Chelsea, weren't you the one who spent half of English class rearranging the letters in the words, 'Rick Debrock' to see if they had a hidden Satanic meaning?"

So then I spent fifteen minutes explaining to Samantha how my mom had assigned me as Adrian's chaperone, and I was on Prohibition patrol. "I need someone to hang out with while I'm there. I mean, I can't be the only one in the room with an iPod strapped to my ears in an attempt to drown out his singing. It would look funny."

Samantha sighed and said she would check and see what Logan was doing. Which meant I couldn't depend on her, since she was obviously using the old, "Let me check and see what my boyfriend has planned" ploy so she could call me back and say, "Darn, but he already bought movie tickets." Like I couldn't see through that. I'd used it myself.

I dialed Aubrie's number. I didn't think I could talk Rachel into coming since she'd been the one to insist that the reason I couldn't find anything suspicious in Rick's name was because I wasn't using his middle name, which was probably something like Damien or Lucifer.

But Aubrie is the friendliest person I know. She doesn't have to fake being peppy while wearing her cheerleading uniform. She was born perky.

Aubrie agreed to come, although she nixed my iPod plan. Then Samantha called back and said that Logan had to work but she could come. Since the three of us were going, I called Rachel and used peer pressure to get her to agree to come with us. As I hung up the phone I thought, this might not be such a drag after all.

The rest of the week passed by in a blur of what had become normal: homework, cheerleading, and ignoring Naomi and her friends. Mom told us that she had to go out of town in two weeks to go to a conference in Arizona on geriatric exercise. Our neighbor, Mrs. Fennelwick, had agreed to check up on us during Mom's absence, and Mom cheerfully reminded us of all the house rules; emphasizing no parties, no boys over, and no pretending that we were lost, dying, or possessed in order to frighten Mrs. Fennelwick. We had already learned by sad experience that Mrs. Fennelwick doesn't have a sense of humor. The story involves a dog whistle, the legend of the ghostly mailman, and her pampered cocker spaniel, but I won't go into that.

Anyway, it was the usual stuff.

Since Mike was likely to show up to Rick's party, I took extra time doing my hair and makeup on Friday night. I have long, strawberry blonde hair. Back before she became princess of the dark, Adrian used to tell me I had the prettiest hair in the world. The first couple of times she dyed her hair, she dyed it strawberry blonde to match mine.

It didn't look right on her though. She doesn't have the blue eyes or the fair coloring that I do. She takes after our dad, with brown hair and dark eyes.

I know people think I'm the prettier sister. You could always tell while we were growing up because my mom's friends would gush about what a beautiful girl I was and then they'd turn to Adrian and say something like, "And my, look how tall you've gotten."

But Adrian is pretty in her own way. I think she has an exotic flare. Well, at least she did before she started smearing so much eyeliner on that it looks like she's trying to pencil in glasses onto her face.

After I'd finished getting ready, I drove Adrian and myself to the Hilltop. She hadn't said much to me since the "Be True to Your School" incident. I'd come home and asked her if she had anything to do with putting Rick's CD into my boom box and she'd said, "You must have accidentally put it in there yourself. Don't blame us for your disorganization."

I could see in her face that she wanted to believe what she'd just said, but didn't. How many excuses would she have to make for Rick before she saw him for what he was? Softly, so she knew I wasn't attacking her, I said, "Adrian, how can you like a guy who's going to spend his entire life getting in trouble?"

Whatever doubt had flickered in her expression immediately extinguished. "Rick is the smartest person I know," she said. "You don't have to worry about him. Or me."

I dropped it after that. I was not about to let her start a lecture on how brilliant Rick was. She liked to point out that he skipped a grade back in elementary school. Big deal. You'd never know it by the way he goofs off in class now.

So anyway, we were pretty silent until we got to the Hilltop and had to park down the street because the parking lot was full. As we walked up to the restaurant she said, "You don't have to drive me home. Rick is going to take me."

"No, Mom said she wanted us to stick together. That means you're going home with me."

Adrian tossed her hair off her shoulder, or at least she would have tossed it if it hadn't been shellacked with so much hair spray that it didn't move. "What are you—Mom, the sequel? You guys can't keep me away from Rick forever. We're in love."

I couldn't help myself; I laughed. I know it wasn't the most sensitive thing to do, but I just couldn't imagine anyone being in love with a guy who changed hair color more often than he changed his socks. I mean, if he couldn't even commit to one shade of hair dye, how was he ever going to commit to a relationship? Adrian shot me a dark look and I removed all traces of humor from my face. "He's told you he loves you?" I couldn't imagine that either.

She didn't answer, which meant he hadn't. Instead she lifted an eyebrow at me in a superior way. "Sometimes you don't have to say it. When you're in love you know it."

We'd almost reached the restaurant doors and I slowed my pace. "You know it? That's all there is to it?"

Her expression softened, as though just talking about Rick improved her mood. "The first time he danced with me, I knew it was love."

How can you take someone seriously who says things like that? "Just because you danced together? Shouldn't other things matter when you make those kinds of decisions?"

She rolled her eyes like I was the one being foolish. "See, that's how I can tell you've never been in love. If you had, you'd understand."

Uh-huh. Some people refuse to be reasonable.

After we went inside, I looked for my friends. This proved to be harder than I thought because the place was packed. Most of the senior class had come, and as Aubrie pointed out when I finally found my friends, quite a few attractive strangers besides.

"Who would have thought that Rick knew hot guys?" Rachel said. "Do you think they're from Moscow or that they're college men?"

Moscow, Idaho, was only eight miles away from Pullman, Washington, so there was always a certain amount of crossover at any given activity. But since the other two Deadbeats in Rick's band went to WSU, it was more likely that the hot guys were their friends.

"Doesn't Rick have an older brother?" Samantha asked.

He did. I knew this because I'd heard Adrian talk about him. Pullman High was so small that normally you knew who everyone was, even in the classes a year or two ahead of you, but Rick moved here the end of our sophomore year. His older brother stayed in California to finish high school, and then came to Pullman to go to WSU after that.

Adrian said he was conceited and obnoxious. I figured that since she thought Rick was normal—whereas I thought Rick scored rather high on the conceited and obnoxious scale—that Rick's older brother must be so bad he had dedicated his life to harassing people in customer service departments.

"I've never seen Rick's older brother," I said, "I'd tell you to watch for someone who looks like Rick, but to tell you the truth under all his hair color and eyeliner, I'm still not sure what Rick looks like."

"Well, at least Rick had the taste to rent out a nice place for his party," Samantha said. "How much do you think it cost him?"

"A lot," Rachel said. "This place isn't cheap."

"Where do you think he got the money?" Aubrie whispered.

"Probably doing something illegal," I said. "That's why he constantly changes his hair. It helps him evade the authorities."

Because Rick had always hung out with the fringe teenagers, and since he'd only lived here for a year and a half, my friends knew very little about him.

"Does his family have money?" Rachel asked, and then everyone looked at me, like I should know. And you would think I would, seeing as Rick was dating my sister. But I didn't. I generally blocked Rick, and all things Rick-like, out of my mind.

Most of the kids at Pullman High had parents who worked at WSU or Schweitzer Engineering Labs, which made us a fairly homogeneous tax-bracket group. I'd just assumed Rick was the same, but now I struggled to remember if there was something different about his background. What had Adrian said about his family?

Um . . . they didn't understand his musical genius . . . and well, I usually stopped listening after that. Could they be wealthy?

Rick drove a jeep. Those weren't that expensive. On the other hand, over the summer his family had vacationed in Kauai. I knew this because Adrian had moped around for the entire two weeks he'd been gone. That's when I'd started trying to set her up with normal guys.

I shrugged. "Maybe they have money."

I didn't say more because Rick walked up to the mike,

welcomed people, and started his first song. I recognized it right away. It was the one we'd accidentally played at the pep assembly. Everyone burst into applause. I rolled my eyes, then let my gaze wander over the crowd.

I mentally rated each outfit I saw, every once in a while commenting to my friends if someone had made a great choice or an especially glaring mistake. Samantha is trying to break me of this habit because she says I sound like a fashion fascist, but really, is it that hard for people to follow simple rules? No one gets mad at teachers for pointing out where you should use punctuation in your writing. It's the same thing, but instead of commas, I point out that you shouldn't wear a sweater that makes you look like you're smuggling a life vest under your shirt.

I want to be a fashion designer someday so I have to pay attention to this kind of stuff. Besides, it's not like I say these things to people's faces. Although I admit I'm considering it in Naomi's case. She's so thin and wears such tight-fitting clothes, that every time I see her I have the urge to slip her a Snickers bar just to keep her from starving to death.

She and Mike were hanging out with the football crowd. The guys smiled and talked with her, accepting her as easily as they ever accepted me. Naomi had her hand draped across Mike's waist in a way that made me feel conspicuously boy-less and wanting to spend the rest of the evening dancing with a hot, mysterious stranger.

In fact I needed it. I wasn't about to go one more night letting Mike think that I was still moping over him.

I leaned over to Rachel. "Hey, are any of the cute guys

here without girlfriends?" I knew she'd know. Rachel calculates these sorts of things almost subconsciously.

"Enough of them to keep me busy," she said.

Samantha's gaze skipped back and forth between the two of us. "I thought we came to keep an eye on Adrian. Is this going to turn into one of those everyone-goes-off-flirting-with-guys-and-I'm-left-standing-by-myself-in-a-corner nights?"

"Maybe," I said.

She rolled her eyes. "I knew I shouldn't have come without Logan."

"I'll stay with you," Aubrie said, "because I'm loyal, and besides, I have too much taste to go out with any of Rick's friends."

"Thanks." Samantha cast me a glance designed to make me feel guilty.

Rachel put her hand on my arm. I recognized the boy-hunting glint in her eye—and yes, she does actually use the term *boy-hunting*. She has a whole hunting-season vocabulary worked out. She smiled at me. "Let's go get a drink and scope out the room." Then she shrugged in Samantha and Aubrie's direction. "Well, we all agreed that Chelsea needs a new boyfriend; and I'm going to let her have first pick."

"All right," Samantha said with a martyr-like sigh. "If it's for a good cause . . ."

How had I suddenly become a pity project?

I followed after Rachel, enjoying the growing distance from Rick's music. Honestly, he only knew one volume: painfully loud.

When we got to the back of the room, we picked up some

sodas and looked around. Out of the corner of my eye, I noticed a tall guy in tan Dockers and a white button-down shirt off to our right. A Hilltop employee. A few guys dressed in the same uniform milled around the room, picking up discarded cups and plates, and in general acting as crowd control.

I ignored him and looked out at the guys standing around the edges of the room.

"The quarry is before us," Rachel said, "so dust off your supply of pickup lines and let's stalk our prey."

"I don't have a supply of pickup lines," I said.

"Then you can use one of mine. Try: Is it hot in here, or is it just you?"

I laughed because I couldn't imagine myself saying that to anyone. My gaze traveled around the room. "They're nice, healthy stock," I said.

"Got anyone in your sights?" Rachel asked.

I didn't answer and kept looking. It only took me half a minute to realize that this wasn't such a good idea after all. I'd forgotten that trying to pick up guys involves the very big possibility of rejection. And did I really need any more of that right now? I think not.

"How about that tall blond guy by the door?" Rachel said. "He's here with a friend but he keeps looking around— a sure sign he wants to meet someone."

When I didn't protest, she nodded in his direction, sizing him up again. "We'll have to approach slowly so as not to scare him off. Blonds startle easily."

I didn't move. I just stood there clutching my glass. "You

know, I'm not sure I want to do this. It's been so long since I've been hunting, I think I've forgotten how to talk to new guys."

Before Rachel could answer, a voice off to my right said, "Oh, I don't know about that. You didn't have any problem talking to me."

I recognized the voice. Even before I turned, I knew the Clark Kent guy stood next to me.

Chapter 6

I gasped and said something that came out as, "Ahh eeh!"
Plus I jumped a little, which jostled the drink in my hand
so that some of it spilled onto the floor. This was especially
bad since he obviously worked here and probably didn't appreciate people sloshing soda around in the restaurant.

"Oh, sorry." I grabbed a few napkins from the table and
bent down to mop up the mess.

"No, it was my fault." He took some more napkins and
bent down to help me. "I shouldn't have spoken like that. I'd
forgotten how easily blondes startle."

I felt myself blush bright red. I'm not sure which embarrassed me more: That I'd run into him again after taking his
money and disappearing, or that he'd heard Rachel and me
discuss hunting guys.

In an attempt to regain some dignity, I stuttered, "Uh,
thanks for your help. With the floor I mean. And also, you
know, the other night."

"You still owe me a dance," he said.

I blinked at him, surprised that he still wanted anything to
do with me. "Do you want to dance right now?"

He glanced at the table. "Sure. Cup cleanup can wait for a few minutes."

I'd forgotten he was working. "We don't have to if it's a problem," I said. "I wouldn't want to get you in trouble."

He grinned. "You're not getting out of our bargain that easily. Remember, I paid for you."

Rachel's jaw dropped, reminding me that I hadn't told her the complete story of how Samantha and I had gotten into the Halloween dance. I'd have to do that soon. In the meantime, I sent her a shrug and followed the guy toward the dance floor.

"I really meant to come back," I said as we walked, "but then I had to leave suddenly." Really suddenly, while being escorted by an angry security guard to the back door. Only I didn't want to admit to that. What would the guy think of me if he knew I'd been kicked out of the dance for disorderly conduct?

He shook his head. "You know, Bo Peep gave me a really bad time because you ditched me."

"I didn't ditch you. It's just a very busy time of year for angels."

Luckily I didn't have to hear his response to that, because Rick started up his next song and it was, as usual, too loud for any conversation and most brain-wave functions. It must be the loudness of the music, after all, that made it so hard to think straight. And also made my stomach feel fluttery this way.

As I danced I told myself not to continually stare at the guy. Which was hard. My gaze kept traveling back to him no matter how hard I tried to find something else to look at. I loved that his dark hair had a hint of curl so it looked like he'd just run his fingers through it. And that he had perfect angular features. And . . .

I made myself look for Adrian. She danced by herself right in front of the band. Her gaze didn't leave Rick, and I noticed for the first time how short her leather skirt was and how the black fishnet stockings she wore made her look ten years older. I'd have to point that out to Mom.

My gaze wandered back to the hot guy and I found him watching me. He smiled and looked away. The fluttering in my stomach spread through my whole body and Adrian's words ran through my mind. "The first time he danced with me, I knew it was love." Was this how Adrian had felt when she looked at Rick?

I dismissed the idea. It was foolishness. It was just because Mike was across the room paying attention to Naomi. Of course I wanted some new guy to notice me. Who wouldn't? There was no such thing as love at first dance. You couldn't really love a person when you knew nothing about him. We probably had nothing in common.

I peered at a wall for a full twenty seconds before my gaze slid back to the guy. Okay, who needed anything in common when a guy had broad shoulders, an easy smile, and Clark Kent blue eyes. I didn't want to just dance with him, I wanted to put on a cape and soar through the sky with him.

I forced myself to look away and take deep breaths. How old was he? He didn't look that much older than me, but it was hard to tell in the low light. If he was a freshman in college—just a year older than me, then maybe he'd still consider dating me. Although, even this felt like hoping for a lot.

As I watched him he turned and saw me staring. He smiled, but I turned away, embarrassed.

Off to my left, Rachel danced with the blond guy we'd been talking about. Further off Mike and Naomi danced, which yeah—who cared about them? Suddenly Mike seemed so young and blasé.

The song ended and the band slid into a slower beat. I didn't think Rick was capable of composing a ballad. So far everything I'd heard vibrating through my bedroom wall had been stuff you could pogo stick to, but he stepped to the mike and said, "We're going to slow things down for a few minutes. This is one of my new songs called, 'The Pretty Girl Curse.'"

Leave it to Rick to come up with a name like that for a slow song.

We stopped dancing and the guy looked over at the band then at me. "Well, I guess your debt to me is paid."

I put my hand on his arm so he wouldn't walk away. "But I accumulated interest. In more than one way."

Another smile. He had great teeth. "Then we should dance some more." He pulled me into slow dance position. I liked the way he smelled subtly of aftershave and how I fit so comfortably against him. I also liked the way he kept looking over at me, as though trying to read something in my face.

The only thing I didn't like was that the music grew so loud again that we couldn't talk. But it was nice standing with him, swaying to the music. I even started to think that Rick was not such a bad singer after all. His voice was sort of melodic when he wasn't using it to screech things.

Then a line in his lyrics caught my attention. "Cheerleading girl—behind the facade, isn't it odd, how ugly is your world." And the song went on, all about how awful cheerleaders were.

I stared up at the stage. "That is so mean."

"What?" the guy asked.

"His lyrics are so rude."

"What?" the guy asked again, and I knew he couldn't hear me.

I shook my head, "Never mind." After all, it was just a stupid song. So who cared that Rick bad-mouthed cheerleaders for one song? His last album had consisted of bad-mouthing the school, the government, and adults in general. Rick apparently didn't like anyone. Big deal.

The song ended but the guy held onto my arm. His eyes caught mine and I was struck again by how familiar they looked. "Do you want to go somewhere that's easier to talk?" he asked.

"Let's go back by the drinks," I answered, because at least I'd been able to understand him there. Besides, I really was worried about his boss getting mad at him for leaving his post. We walked to the back of the room while Rick started up his next song, entitled, "We Don't Need Your Sis-Boom-Bah Crap." This song consisted mostly of swear words.

"Unbelievable. Rick is absolutely unbelievable," I said.

"That's why I listen to country," the guy said.

I laughed and tried to shake off my irritation. "Yeah, country songs don't criticize cheerleaders."

He nodded, "You know, there are strikingly few country songs about cheerleaders. But maybe one day they'll find their rightful place in music lore with bootleggers and coal miners."

Which is when I decided not to tell the guy I was a cheerleader. Right then I wanted to be older, intellectual, and dripping with sophistication.

He tilted his head at me. "So if you're not a Rick and the Deadbeats fan, what are you doing here?"

"Watching my little sister. See, sadly she was born without the gene for taste or common sense and so she likes Rick's music. I only came to make sure there wasn't any alcohol here." As soon as I said this, I realized I'd insulted him. After all, he worked here.

I tried to backpedal. "Not that I'm saying you'd give alcohol to minors."

Instead of being angry he just laughed. "Yeah, high school kids don't need liquor to make them act like idiots." He nodded up at some of Rick's friends who were jumping around and slamming into one another. "They can do that on hormones alone."

He said this as if he didn't think of me as a high school student. Which made sense. He'd seen me up on campus first. Was there a way I could pull off being a college student? Maybe live a double life just so he'd be interested in me? I was willing to consider it.

He looked over across the crowd. "So your little sister goes to Pullman High?"

"Yeah." It wasn't a lie. Okay, he probably assumed she was

a senior since most of Rick's friends were, but technically it wasn't a lie.

Out on the dance floor I noticed Samantha and Aubrie talking. Samantha kept shaking her head and Aubrie had her hand covering her mouth. Which meant they were listening to the anti-cheerleader lyrics of Rick's song too.

Adrian still stood in the front of the room by the band, swinging her hips to the music. My own sister was dancing to Rick ripping on cheerleaders. It seemed like she should have stuck up for me—or at least warned me. I mean, his new CD had two anti-cheerleading songs on it?

I glanced back at the guy and saw him watching me. I'd never lied about my age before, but looking at his eyes made me seriously consider doing it.

"I'm sorry I keep staring at you," he said. "It's just that you remind me of someone." He looked down at the floor and shook his head. "You probably think that's a pickup line, don't you? You're going to put that into your supply along with the 'Is it hot or is it just you' line."

"No," I said. "Well—just as long as I remind you of someone who's pretty."

"Gorgeous," he said. "Stunning."

"See, that's much better than the 'Are you hot' line. Who do you think I look like?"

He shook his head. "I can't put my finger on it. That's what bothers me."

I took a step closer to him. "At this point most guys would just throw out the name of an impressive celebrity."

He laughed and leaned toward me. "I'm not making it up. You really do remind me of someone. Do you believe that?"

I nodded. "Actually when I first saw you I thought you looked familiar too."

His gaze grew more intense. "Maybe we've met before. Do you work on campus?"

"No." I doubted we'd ever met because I would have remembered him. I've got a good memory where good-looking guys are concerned.

The second song ended. It had been a short one. Probably because it's hard to find words that rhyme with curses. The music started up for the next one and Rick walked to the mike. "This is the song I'm going to sing for the auditions of *High School Idol*. I hope you'll all come out to support me as I rock to *Dangerously Blonde*."

"We must have met somewhere," the guy said. "What's your name?"

I hardly heard him because Rick sang the first verse of his song.

> *Chelsea is so pretty—*
> *Every hair is in its place.*
> *Lipstick adds a perfect smile*
> *To her perfect face.*
> *Yes, she's dangerously blonde.*

The breath went out of my lungs. My heart slammed into my ribs. This song was about me. And although he'd called me pretty, he'd said the word like it was an insult. Time froze as I waited for the chorus of his song.

The guy stepped closer to me. "You do have a name, don't you?"

But I couldn't answer. I couldn't even talk. My gaze was stuck on the stage.

> *She'll wink at you, but*
> *Only if you're cool.*
> *Yeah, she knows what she needs to be.*
> *It's all about pop-u-lar-ity,*
> *When you're dangerously blonde.*

"Are you okay?" the guy asked.

I had never been a violent person, but I wanted to wrestle the mike out of Rick's hands and club him with it. How could he do this to me in front of the entire senior class? Why did I deserve this?

The worst part of the whole thing was that—whereas most of Rick's songs sounded like they were wandering around in search of a melody—this song was catchy. It sounded like something you'd hear on the radio. People, people who went to my high school, clapped along. My sister was one of them.

It hurt to swallow. In another moment I would break into a thousand pieces. I turned to the guy, but only for a second. "I've got to go."

"Right now?" he asked.

"Sorry." I walked past him, making my way around the refreshment table.

"What's your name, at least," he asked, but I was not about to tell him my name was Chelsea when Rick was up in front of the room slandering it.

"Sorry," was all I could get out and I hurried away from him.

I took a deep breath. I had to make it to the door without bursting into tears or finding something to hurl at Rick. I could do this.

I would have to leave Adrian here. I wasn't about to walk up to the stage in front of everyone and cause a scene by trying to haul my sister away. It was bad enough that Rick had set his disdain for me to music. I wouldn't make it worse by showing everyone how it affected me.

I had just gone out the door when my friends caught up to me. Even Rachel came, which meant she had left the blond guy to talk to me.

Aubrie hurried to my side. "Chelsea, are you all right?"

"No," I said, and then the tears I'd held back spilled over anyway. I couldn't see but kept walking toward the parking lot.

"He's such a jerk," Aubrie said, and then Rachel added several more adjectives, most of which Rick had already set to music in songs about us.

Samantha glanced over her shoulder at the restaurant to make sure we were alone. "We need to go somewhere and talk. We can't let him do this to Chelsea. What if Rick actually makes it through the *High School Idol* auditions? We can't let him sing that song on national TV."

"How are we going to stop him?" I asked.

She looked around the group and then gazed at me. "I think you already know the answer to that question."

I held up my hands, using them to ask the question. "We cough on him and give him laryngitis?"

"No, Chels, you've got to sing. You've got to beat him at the auditions."

Chapter 7

We drove to Samantha's house, then sat cross-legged in her bedroom discussing the details.

"You still have two weeks to memorize a song. It will be easy," Samantha said. "You memorized 'Be True to Your School' without even trying."

"But Rick wrote his own song. How can I top that?"

Rachel waved off my question, like it was silly. "You're better looking and have nice legs. You don't think Britney Spears got where she is because she wrote her songs, do you?"

Aubrie considered me with her head tilted. "You'll need something sparkly to wear. Something that looks rock star. We'll look on the Internet."

"What if the *High School Idol* judges are mean?" I asked. "They chew people up and spit them out on those reality shows. I don't want the whole nation making fun of me because I forget a word, or drop a note, or pass out during the audition. I don't know if I can do this."

"Sure you can," Aubrie said. "We'll be your backup singers."

Samantha and Rachel shot her angry looks. Clearly, they were less than thrilled with the idea of being my backup singers.

"Oh come on," Aubrie said. "We do dances all the time. It will be just like one of our pep assembly routines."

"Except for potentially performing in front of millions of viewers," Rachel said.

Samantha let out a sigh. "Aubrie is right. We're in this together. Rick didn't just attack Chelsea. He wrote at least two songs about cheerleaders and who knows how many more that we didn't hear. Maybe he'll sing about all of us tonight. He wants to take us on, I say we make sure his stupid songs never see the light of day. It will be our revenge."

"Revenge of the cheerleaders," Rachel said, and we nodded in agreement.

After that we spent the next hour on the Internet. We looked at dozens of songs, trying to find something that was in my vocal range, with a good dance beat, and recognizable but not played out. I wanted to find a song about evil band members entitled "Dangerously Stupid," but apparently nobody has written that song yet.

Finally, and after much discussion, we chose Cher's "The Shoop Shoop Song (It's in His Kiss)." It was fun, bouncy, and had a strong backup part. And besides, the words seemed easy to memorize.

I only had to sing a few lines before my friends came in with their response, and then so much of the song worked like a conversation.

Not really all that frightening if you took out the part where we had to do it in front of people.

"I'll sign us up for the audition," Aubrie said.

"I'll ask Mrs. Jones to help us come up with a routine," Rachel added.

"What do you want me to do?" I asked.

Samantha let out a sigh. "Remember when you quit choir, you were so glad you never had to sing for Mr. Metzerol again?"

"Yeah," I said. I knew what she was going to say, and dreaded it before she opened her mouth again.

"Go ask him if he can coach you through the song."

∽ ∽ ∽

When I got home my mother asked me where Adrian was. I told her I didn't care because I was never speaking to Adrian again, and then, even though I thought I had finished crying, I cried all over again when I told my mother what had happened.

Mom listened, shaking her head. "How could he do such a thing?" she asked. "What's wrong with him?" And then finally she threw her hands up and said, "Well, that's the last straw. Adrian is not seeing that boy anymore. He is no longer welcome in our home."

An hour later Adrian came home. By that time I was up in the bathroom brushing my teeth. I heard Mom's voice, low and angry, talking to my sister, and then Adrian's voice, louder and defensive, saying, "It's just a song. Besides, she insults him all the time."

"That isn't the same," Mom said. "You know that isn't the same."

Something slammed. Probably the coat closet. "How come you always take her side?"

"And how come you never do?" Mom snapped back. "She's your sister. And until Rick apologizes to Chelsea and promises not to sing that song, you won't see him. Is that clear?"

I heard footsteps storming down the hall then Adrian yelled, "You're trying to ruin my life!"

As if she needed any help doing that.

Adrian walked by the bathroom and saw me rinsing out my toothbrush. She paused by the doorway, her breath still coming out quickly. "So now you're taking Rick away from me."

"I didn't make him sing that song."

"But you told Mom about it. You blew it all out of proportion. It's not like he said anything that isn't true."

I stared at her, then shook my head. How could she see things that way? How could she have so much hatred for me that she thought her boyfriend was justified in singing trash about me in front of everybody? At that moment I wanted to hurt her as badly as she hurt me. With an even voice I said, "Tell me, how many songs did Rick write about you on his new CD?"

"What?" she asked.

"Did he write any songs about what a wonderful girl-friend you are?"

She let out an exasperated grunt, "The CD is called *Cheerleaders in Action*. I'm not a cheerleader."

"Oh. Well doesn't it seem a little obsessive that your boyfriend wrote a bunch of songs about your sister? Maybe you should think about that."

When her face flushed red I knew my words had hit their mark. Still, she wasn't going to let me have the last word in the argument. She took a step toward me. "Rick isn't interested in you. He wrote those songs about cheerleaders because he's sick of watching the way you and your friends walk over everyone else."

As if. I would have loved to hear about just who she thought I'd been waltzing over, but I wasn't about to let myself get distracted. Instead I shrugged, "So you're saying he does think you're a wonderful girlfriend?"

She lifted her chin as though daring me to contradict her. "Yes. He loves me."

"Well, since he doesn't want to lose you, he shouldn't have a hard time apologizing to me and switching songs for the audition, should he?"

She rolled her eyes. "You don't think he'll do it? You think you've gotten rid of him just because you told Mom about that song? Well, even though you've never apologized to him for the way you look down at him all the time, and even though 'Dangerously Blonde' is his best song, he'll do it if I ask him to."

I smiled at her. "Mmm hmm. Why don't you go call him now?"

Even though I didn't show any confidence in her assertion,

I really did hope she was right. And I didn't even care about the apology. I just wanted him to never sing that song again. If he would promise not to sing it, that would mean I didn't have to shove myself into something tight and sparkly and sing "The Shoop Shoop Song" in front of heaven knew how many people.

Adrian went into her room and shut the door. I leaned against her door frame and tried to hear as much of the conversation as I could. Was there a sparkly outfit in my future or not?

Adrian, sniffling, told Rick about Mom's edict. She ended with, "It isn't fair to you. I know it isn't, but can you please tell them that you won't sing that song again?"

There was a moment's silence then Adrian said, "But you have other songs—you have tons of other songs you can perform."

A pause, then Adrian's voice grew louder. "Does your artistic freedom mean more to you than seeing me?"

Another pause. "Well, it must if you're not willing to sing a different song."

Now her voice grew choppy with anger. "I can't believe this. Chelsea told me you wouldn't change songs, but I didn't believe her. You don't love me at all, do you?"

Hardly a pause. Whatever Rick said, she cut him off. "Fine, then I don't care if I never see you again. And another thing, Rick, how is it that you wrote a whole CD worth of songs about my sister and not a single one about me?"

She didn't give him time to answer. Even from where I stood I could hear the phone slam against her desk.

I turned and walked slowly back to my room. Funny how things turn out sometimes. Adrian finally was free from all Rick's bad influences, but me, well, I was going to have to face him head-on. I lay in bed, but didn't fall asleep for a long time. The words of "Dangerously Blonde" repeated over and over again in my mind.

ᔕ ᔕ ᔕ

I spent most of Saturday at Rachel's house with my friends, practicing the song and combing through Internet sites trying to find outfits that were flashy but not slutty. As it turns out, those are very expensive. We found some dresses that would be perfect, and which could be mailed to us on time for a mere one hundred and eighty dollars apiece. I think they may have originally been figure skating outfits, but hey, they were sparkly and looked liked they'd stay put on your body even if you did leg kicks. Trust me, those are hard to find.

At noon we went over to Mrs. Jones's house. Rachel had called her in the morning and she'd agreed to give us an hour of her time to help us do some choreography. The hour stretched into three hours, which was really nice of Mrs. Jones, since I'm sure she's very busy doing whatever it is that teachers do on the weekends.

By the time I finally went home I felt confident. Confident about the routine, confident about the outfits, confident that my friends could pull off the backup part—the only thing I didn't feel confident about was my singing voice.

"You have potential," Mr. Metzerol had told me back when I'd taken choir. "But potential must be shaped."

Instead of shaping my potential by joining show choir, like he wanted, I'd dropped the class altogether this year. I knew he was disappointed in me. Whenever he passed me in the hallway his gaze revealed his sense of betrayal.

If I asked him, would he agree to help me or would he just rub it in that my potential was still a massive unshaped blob?

∽ ∽ ∽

Monday at school things were worse than I expected. I'd known a lot of people had heard Rick's songs, but I hadn't expected so many people to be singing them in the hallway. Really. I caught snatches of it every time I switched classes. Naomi and her friends broke into, "She'll wink at you, but only if you're cool," whenever they saw me.

I tried to laugh it off and tell them, "You notice I'm not winking at you. You obviously didn't make the cool list." But it still bothered me. I mean, how far could a person's social standing slide in one weekend? It was like anyone who I'd ever slighted, every guy I'd ever turned down, and all the girls who tried out but didn't make it on the cheerleading squad went out of the way to rub it in.

From what I gathered—from those who were only too eager to tell me—Rick sang a couple more cheerleader songs after we left. There was "How to Feed Your Cheerleader (On Gossip and Lies)" and "This Skirt Means I'm Too Good for

You." Apparently they were catchy tunes because several people had them almost memorized.

The other girls in my squad weren't nearly as bothered by it as I was. Samantha had a lot of noncheerleading friends and a boyfriend. Every time Logan passed Rick in the hallway he called out, "Heck yeah, she's too good for you! That's why she's dating me."

Rachel had come to school looking so forlorn that currently half a dozen guys from the football team trailed her around to cheer her up and snarl in Rick's direction.

Aubrie, eternally optimistic, actually enjoyed the extra attention. "There is no bad press," she said. I didn't point out that this only applied to movie stars, not high school students. At high school—oh yeah, there's bad press.

By lunchtime I knew I could no longer avoid it. I went to Mr. Mezterol's classroom to see if I could talk to him. He was there, standing by his filing cabinet going through sheet music. He wore a suit jacket and tie—I'd never seen him in anything casual, and his mustache was neatly trimmed. I used to think his mustache was actually a word filter because he always spoke so slowly. He told his classes that when conversing, it was important to choose exactly the right word, and you did get the feeling that he ran through a mental thesaurus every time he spoke. He looked up when I walked in, but then went back to his filing.

I stood before him, nervously clutching a CD of the song that I'd downloaded last night, and explained that I was trying out for the *High School Idol* auditions. I needed help with my voice. Did he have any time to offer me some pointers?

He turned, slowly, and considered me with reproach. "I'm not sure, Chelsea. Many of my choir students are trying out, and I need to help them. My time is very limited over the next two weeks. You understand that my choir students have first priority."

I gulped, and grabbed my CD harder, but didn't leave. He had started his answer by saying, "I'm not sure," which meant he could still be persuaded. "But it won't take long," I said. "And I used to be your student. How about I'll stay after school and help you grade papers so you'll have extra time. Or I could clean your classroom, or wash your car . . ." Or just grovel for a sufficient time for you to forgive me. "Please?"

He looked at me for a long moment, tapping his fingers against the sheet music in his hand. "Perhaps we could work out a deal. After all, I shouldn't turn down someone who's . . ." His mustache twitched. "Inspired so much music lately."

I blushed. "You heard about Rick's song?"

He turned back to his filing cabinet and placed the last piece of sheet music in the drawer. "Some girls in my second period class sung several songs to me. That 'Dangerously Blonde' one has a good beat."

I leaned against his desk. "Now you know why I've got to sing really well. I can't let Rick win a spot on *High School Idol.*"

"Mmm hmm." Mr. Metzerol shut the file then made his way around to the back of his desk. He sat down in his chair and clasped his hands in front of him. "It's a brutal thing to be on the wrong end of teasing, isn't it?"

"Yes," I said, glad that he understood.

"School should be a place of learning, of friendship, but words . . ." he shook his head sadly, "those take a toll on a person's self-esteem, wouldn't you agree?"

"Yes," I said.

The corners of his mouth lifted, as though winning an argument. "It's so important to feel accepted by one's peers."

I'd already said as much, so I wasn't sure why he kept bringing it up. "You don't think I pick on people, do you?" I put my hand against my chest. "Because those things Rick said about me aren't true."

He didn't look convinced. "You try to include your peers whenever you can?"

"Yes." I should have seen it coming, really. I mean, I'd used the same put-your-money-where-your-mouth-is technique on Adrian.

"Then you won't mind helping me with a project. You're the perfect one to do it, in fact, since you know how it feels to be on the wrong end of teasing." He leaned back in his chair and stroked the ends of his mustache. "You see, I'm worried about a couple of my students, Molly and Polly Patterson. You know them, yes?"

Yes, I knew them. They were identical twin girls who'd moved into town this year and had the misfortune of being plain, frumpy, and on the overweight side. They'd immediately been dubbed Roly and Poly by some guys on the football team. "They're in my history class," I said.

"That's right," Mr. Metzerol said. "They have choir first period. Superb voices. Excellent harmony. I can't get either one to sing a solo though. They're too self-conscious. Too worried about what others might say."

"You want me to help them with singing?" I asked.

Mr. Metzerol leaned forward. "I want you to help them with life at PHS. I want you to be their friend."

"Oh." Adults love to say these kinds of things as though you could order friendship the same way you ordered a pizza. You didn't just decide to be friends with two people whom you'd hardly ever spoken to and probably had nothing in common with. Still, I couldn't explain this to Mr. Metzerol. Once people become adults they instantly forget what it's like to be a teenager.

Mr. Metzerol nodded appraisingly. "If they hang out with you, people will stop making fun of them."

Yeah, because they'd be too busy making fun of me. My popularity was already in a free fall. Thank you very much, Rick.

Still I couldn't turn Mr. Metzerol down. I needed his help, and besides, he was right. I knew how it felt to be called names. "I'll try to get to know them. I'll say hi in class and everything if you want me to."

"Yes, but we need . . ." He sat silently at his desk while I waited for him to finish his sentence. "Something . . . more." And then, as though it were already decided he added, "I'll take the liberty of asking Mrs. Addington to put the three of you together on your history project. That should give you an opportunity to become friends."

We were just starting a unit on technology in world history class and had to come up with a report and presentation.

"But Samantha and I already decided to do our project together . . ." I said.

"Good, good," he said. "Samantha can help you befriend them. That will work out even better. I'll let Mrs. Addington know." He stood up as though the matter was closed. "Now then, you brought your music with you? Let's hear it."

I didn't argue with him anymore. As far as I was concerned, if he made me befriend Molly and Polly he had better give me a lot of good coaching advice in return.

I put my CD into the player that sat on his desk, took a deep breath, and belted out the song.

Mr. Metzerol watched me, frowning the entire time. When I finished he shook his head like a doctor examining a dying patient. "Chelsea, you're not utilizing your diaphragm. You're letting notes fall off left and right." He held his fingers together as though grasping something. "You've got to hold onto those notes." Then he sung out the words to a couple of lines in a booming, almost operatic voice. He nodded at me. "Now try it again without the CD. I want to hear you, not the CD."

I sang the song again, struggling to remember the words while concentrating on my diaphragm. Apparently I wasn't successful with that last goal because Mr. Metzerol kept yelling, "Hold onto it!" and "You're letting those notes fall!" and "God gave you a diaphragm, Chelsea! When are you going to use it?" He even took his conducting stick and held it to my stomach. "Here. Here is where you need to feel it. Stretch those notes out."

Which made me remember why I didn't take choir this

year. The man was not above walking by and smacking us in the back if we slouched during practice, and he had this Nazi-like obsession with making us use our diaphragm.

After the fourth time through the song—both his fourth time and mine, because he had to keep showing me how it should be done—he finally said, "That's enough practice for today. You do your scales and your breathing exercises to-night, then come back in at lunchtime tomorrow and we'll see if it goes any better, all right?"

"All right," I said.

"And remember you're going to help Molly and Polly with . . ." Mr. Metzerol rolled his hand in the air, pumping his mental thesaurus. "Updating their look. Building their confidence."

As though you could just walk up to near strangers and say, Hi, I noticed you're ugly. Would you like some help with that? Honestly, Mr. Metzerol must have skipped out on his teenage years. "I'll try," I said. "I can't promise anything."

He sent me a calm smile. "Then neither can I."

You wouldn't think a teacher would blackmail you like that.

Chapter 8

I met up with my friends on the main stairway, affectionately called Jock's Landing because all the jocks hang out there.

"Where were you at lunch?" Aubrie asked.

"I went to Mr. Metzerol's to get some voice coaching."

She blinked in concern. "Do you think the rest of us should go in and see him too?"

"Only if you want to subject yourself to an angry little man repeatedly poking you in the stomach."

I leaned over to Samantha, who wasn't paying attention to me because she was talking to Logan. "Hey, I hope you don't mind, but since Mr. Metzerol is helping me with my singing, he's arranging to have us do our history project with Molly and Polly Patterson." And then I added a little more tentatively, "Mr. Metzerol wants us to be friendly to them, you know, help them fit in at PHS."

Samantha shrugged. "Okay." Then she went back to talking with Logan.

At that moment I really respected Samantha. She wasn't at all concerned about having to hang out with Molly and

Polly or how their lack of popularity would affect us. Which made me feel worse that my own first reaction had been different.

She'll wink at you but only if you're cool . . .

It wasn't true, was it?

I took a deep breath. First reactions didn't define a person. It's what you did—how you acted around others—that was important, and I'd said I'd be friendly to Molly and Polly. So Rick wasn't right about me.

In world history class Mrs. Addington called us up to her desk in groups. Earlier we'd submitted our report topics for her approval.

She called Molly, Polly, Samantha, and me up to her desk last. "Now then," she said with a smile, "I know you didn't request to work together, but since Molly and Polly are still fairly new here, I thought it would be a good idea to put you all in a group together." She looked directly at me. "That's all right with you, isn't it?"

I smiled back at her. "Sure."

Samantha nodded. "That's fine."

Molly and Polly glanced at each other and then suspiciously at us. "I guess that's okay," Molly said. At least I think it was Molly. I couldn't really tell them apart. They both had mousy brown hair pulled back in ponytails and identical wire-rimmed glasses.

Mrs. Addington said, "Great. I'll let you guys get to the library and decide whether you want to work on . . ." She peered down at a paper on her desk. "The history of space flight or inventions that spurred on the industrial revolution. They're both good topics."

We picked up our books and left the room. While we walked in the hallway, Molly and Polly kept two paces ahead of us, talking together and glancing back at us.

"Remember," I whispered to Samantha, "we're supposed to give them some pointers about fitting in here."

We reached the library door and Molly and Polly stopped to face us. "Look, you can be in our group," Molly said. "But we're doing the report on space flight, and we're not letting you cheat off of us." Then they pushed the library doors open and walked in.

We stood there in the hallway staring after them. "Well," Samantha finally said. "I just thought of their first pointer for fitting in."

I folded my arms. "Because we're cheerleaders we're automatically cheaters?"

"Shhh," Samantha said. "You don't want to give Rick any more song ideas."

We walked into the library, put our books on a table with Molly's and Polly's, then went and found books on space exploration, all of which, I'd like to point out, looked so boring they could be officially classified as sleep aids. We took notes, and in between jotting down things about *Sputnik* and Neil Armstrong I tried to make small talk with our new study partners. At first they answered all of my questions coldly, like they were just waiting for me to be rude, but after fifteen minutes they loosened up.

Molly kept saying snarky asides that made me laugh. "If they can put a man on the moon, why can't they put them all there?" And, "Well, of course the Soviets made it to space first. They were Russian."

She was as bitingly funny as Polly was tenderhearted. Polly kept ohhhing and ahhhing over the pictures of Laika the first astronaut dog.

And yes, in case you didn't know, they really did send a dog orbiting around the earth. Or as Molly pointed out, not only the Russians, but the canines, beat us into space.

When class was nearly over, I said, "Some of us are getting together to go to the movies this weekend. Do you want to come?"

"Who are 'us'?" Molly asked.

"I'm not sure about everyone who's going," I said, because I'd just planned this off the top of my head and hadn't actually asked anyone. "Samantha and I—"

"And Logan," Samantha said.

"Right, and Logan . . . Aubrie, Rachel—whoever Rachel is currently stringing along in her football harem—"

"Sorry," Polly said. "We don't . . . um . . ." She glanced at her sister.

"Go anywhere near football players unless we're forced to by teachers or natural disasters," Molly finished.

Polly leaned over to her sister. "Not all the football players are bad."

Molly rolled her eyes, then turned her attention back to me. "Is Joe Diaz going to be there?"

Joe was a wide receiver, and not a bad one at that, although it was his twin brother, Garret, who got the most attention on the team. Garret was the quarterback. Plus, Garret had this tall-dark-and-handsome thing going for him. Joe and Garret weren't identical twins though, and Joe, well, Joe was just tall and dark.

"I could invite him if you wanted," I volunteered.

"No," Polly said quickly. "No, that would be awkward. If he wanted to talk to me again he would have by now."

"Again?" Samantha asked. Her voice had a tell-me-more lilt to it.

When Polly didn't volunteer any more information, Molly leaned forward, conspiratorially. "They once had a ten-minute conversation in English about why being a twin is the pits."

"It was nothing personal," Polly told her sister.

"Yeah, I'll remember that if you ever need a kidney," Molly said.

I shrugged at Polly. "Maybe he just needs an opportunity to talk to you again. Why don't you come with us to the movies, and I'll invite some of the guys—"

"No, I can't." Polly held up both hands to stop me. "I get nosebleeds when I'm nervous. Really bad. In my last school they called me A+ Polly—and they weren't talking about my grade point average. This school is already bad enough. I don't need any more nicknames."

Samantha said, "You shouldn't let a few names stop you from doing what you want."

"You just need some confidence," I said. "Hanging out with friends is nothing to get nervous about."

You would have thought I'd just told Polly to fly. She

looked at me in total disbelief. "No offense, but it's easy for you to have confidence. You're both . . ." She waved a hand in our general direction. "Cheerleaders. You don't know what it means to have people make fun of you."

Which made me laugh out loud. "We don't just have nicknames," I said. "We've got an entire CD dedicated to us."

Molly shook her head. "Yeah, but those songs are about how cheerleaders think they're better than everyone else. In the long run they'll probably just make you more attractive to high school guys. No one has ever accused us of thinking we're better than everyone else. How do you get that gig?"

I guess it was the fashion designer in me, but without thinking I said, "If you lost the sweatshirts and stood up straight every once in a while you'd find out."

"What?" Polly said.

Samantha put her hand over her face. She'd heard me give enough critiques that she knew where I was going with this.

"Those sweats aren't slimming. They actually add bulk. You need to get some shirts that taper in at the waist. Also your hair doesn't add anything when you just pull it back like that. Hair should frame your face, give it some lift and balance. Your hair isn't doing its job."

Molly and Polly both stared at me with their mouths slightly ajar. Since they weren't talking I figured I'd just finish off my critique. "And a good makeover would help. You're in high school. It's okay to wear makeup."

Molly let out a grunt. "You think a makeover would change anything? We slap on some mascara and suddenly guys stop calling us names and ask for our phone number?"

I said, "If I slouched around in sweats and didn't do my hair or makeup, I wouldn't be dating anyone—well, okay, actually I'm *not* dating anyone, but you know what I mean." I sat back in my chair and surveyed them. "Why don't you let Samantha and me do makeovers on you? We could go clothes shopping too. It would be fun."

Samantha snapped her fingers while she thought. "I bet we could get them in at the salon with Dotti." To the twins she said, "That woman can work miracles with highlights and a haircut."

"Wait a minute." Molly held up one hand. "Suddenly we're talking scissors?"

I nodded. "And you ought to consider contacts. You have really pretty eyes."

Polly touched the frames of her glasses and looked back at me wistfully. "You honestly think so?"

Molly elbowed her sister before I could answer. "Contacts are little pieces of plastic that people shove into their eyes. Hello, that won't feel good."

"Doing a makeover would be lots of fun," Samantha said. "Chelsea's really good at picking out clothes."

Molly and Polly glanced at each other again. It made me wonder if all those stories about twins and telepathy were true because I could almost see the communication passing between them. Polly teetered on the edge of indecision, but Molly stood firm. She said, "It won't make a difference, and if we let them start changing things now, they'll do something awful like rip out half our eyebrows."

I nodded. "You do need a wax job on your eyebrows, yes."

"See," Molly said. "And when it's all said and done nothing will change except my eyebrows will be sore for a week."

And people on TV always seem so excited and grateful when someone offers them a makeover. How was it that I'd run into the two people on the planet who didn't want one? "If I can prove that makeovers make a difference, will you agree to have one?" I asked.

The class bell rung. Everyone around us gathered up their books but none of us moved. "Well?" I asked.

Molly looked at me doubtfully. "How are you going to prove it?"

"Meet Samantha and me after school and we'll run an experiment," I said.

As we went to our next class, I explained the experiment to Samantha. Then she explained why she didn't want to be my friend anymore, but I knew she was just kidding.

After school I waited for everyone by Samantha's car. Samantha and Logan were the first to appear. Logan kept shaking his head as he walked up. "I leave you alone for one night and you join a rock group," he told Samantha. "Now we're apart for a few hours and you're running experiments on how to pick up guys?"

"Well, yeah," she said, "but you don't have to worry because I'm going to be the ugly one who doesn't get picked up."

"It's all in the name of science," I added.

Logan glared at me, then returned his attention to Samantha. "How are you making yourself ugly?"

"I'm going to take all of my makeup off, pull my hair back, wear your sweatshirt, and borrow some glasses."

"And that's going to do it?" he said. "That's your secret ugly disguise?"

"Right," she said.

He shook his head. "I've seen you without makeup and with your hair pulled back. I hate to break this to you, but a sweatshirt and a pair of glasses are not going to make you ugly."

Samantha took a step closer to him and a smile slid across her face. "You're so sweet."

He looked like he was about to kiss her, which frankly I see enough of and which I shouldn't have to endure because I have no boyfriend. I made shooing motions in his direction. "Yes, it's wonderful that love is blind, but stop trying to ruin my experiment. She's supposed to be acting self-conscious and insecure, not radiant."

Logan didn't kiss Samantha, but he did take hold of her hand. "Where are you running this experiment? I may want to stop by and pick you up."

"Campus," I said. "Northside Marketplace."

Logan's head snapped up. "You're going to pick up college guys?"

"Well, we can't very well pick up high school guys," I said. "Everyone at PHS knows who we are."

"Then go to Moscow," he said. "College guys only want one thing from girls, and I'm not talking about the answers to tomorrow's homework."

I scanned the parking lot for the Patterson twins but didn't see them. "It's just easier and faster to go to campus. But don't worry. Samantha isn't going to pick up anyone, and I'm giving out a fake name. For the experiment, I'm Juliet."

Logan shook his head some more, looked at me like I was crazy, then gave Samantha's hand a squeeze. "Give me a call when you're done not picking up men." He bent down and gave her a kiss which I pretended not to see, then left for his own car. Samantha watched him go with a sigh.

"Oh, stop being radiant," I told her. "You'll mess up my experiment."

She didn't stop though. She stood there smiling until Molly and Polly walked up. As we drove to campus, I turned around in my seat and explained the whole premise to the twins.

"Samantha generally attracts a lot of attention from guys," I said. "And do you know why that is?"

"Because she looks like a Barbie doll?" Polly asked.

"No," I said, "because she takes care of herself. She dresses nicely, does her hair and makeup, and has an air of confidence about her. She walks with good posture, and looks up and smiles at the world. People can tell she feels good about who she is."

"And she looks like a Barbie doll," Molly said.

"I don't look like a Barbie doll," Samantha said.

"Anyway," I went on, "if you don't project that image, you don't earn the respect of the male species. Men are like birds that way. They're both attracted to shiny things. And to prove this point, we're going to set Samantha at a table without all of those things we just talked about. You'll see that the guys don't give her a second glance." Molly stared back at me skeptically. I could tell she didn't believe me but I continued with my explanation.

"After a few minutes I'm going to sit down a little ways away from Samantha. I have my makeup on, my hair done, and I'm wearing a nice outfit. I'm going to look up and smile at people, projecting an image of self-confidence. We'll see how long it takes until someone sits down and starts up a conversation with me."

Samantha pulled into a parking lot and turned off the car. "And if Chelsea proves her point, you two agree to have makeovers, okay?"

"Okay," Polly said, then shot her sister a look. "Well, you said you'd do it if she could prove her point."

Molly grunted and opened her car door. "It's not going to work. The reason the guys at high school are mean to us has nothing to do with what we wear or how confident we look. They're mean because they're jerks. I'll watch your experiment, but if it doesn't go how you say it will, then PHS is made up of a bunch of troglodytes, and you should agree to shun every guy who's ever called us Roly or Poly." Molly held out her hand. "Agreed?"

Samantha shook her hand. "Agreed." Which just goes to show Samantha had no idea how many people at PHS had said the words Roly and Poly while describing the Patterson twins. If we lost, we would no longer be mingling with a large segment of the football team.

We walked across the parking lot and onto campus, past streams of students and ancient brick buildings. Samantha slipped Logan's sweatshirt over her top as we walked. "Now, since Chelsea isn't really trying to pick up anyone, you guys will need to go rescue her about a minute after anyone sits down next to her. Just walk up and say, 'Hey Juliet, are you going to English class? We don't want to be late.' Then she'll excuse herself, and we'll all head back to the car." Samantha shot me a firm look. "Right?"

"Right," I said.

She nodded knowingly. "Just don't revise the plan if the guy who happens to sit down next to you is cute, okay? I mean I know you're on the lookout for a new guy and that since things went south with Mike it might be tempting to receive attention from some college hottie, but the last thing you need is a twenty-two-year-old grad student hitting on you."

"Don't worry," I said.

Samantha nudged Molly and in a lower voice said, "If it's a cute guy, Chelsea will last approximately two minutes before she gives out her name, phone number, and e-mail address. In that case, you'll have to go in for an intervention and pull her out for her own good."

"Okay," Molly said.

"I am not that bad," I said.

In a voice that was meant to appease me, Samantha said, "Right. And you don't want to make the rest of us sit around on campus while you flirt with some new conquest."

I rolled my eyes at her, because really, I'm not like that.

I turned to Polly when the Northside Marketplace was in sight. "When we get there, Samantha will need to wear your glasses."

Polly touched her frames tentatively. "But I can't see without them."

"It's part of Samantha's outfit. If you wear them, so should she."

Polly grumbled about this and Molly said it was going to be the blonde leading the blind, but in the end Polly handed them over to Samantha. "Oh all right, Molly will just have to tell me what's happening since it will all be blurry to me."

We walked inside the Northside Marketplace, then Molly and Polly sauntered into the dining room to do reconnaissance while Samantha and I went into the restroom. Samantha went in to wash off all of her makeup and pull her hair back. I went to touch up mine and give Samantha last-minute instructions.

"This whole theory will be blown if some guy sits next to you, so try to look extra repulsive. You know, if anyone comes too near, start spitting or something."

Samantha splashed water from the sink onto her face and didn't answer me.

I ran my fingers through my hair. "And what will we do if no one sits down by me? I mean, it's possible that every guy who comes by will already be seeing someone, or shy, or just not interested." My hands nearly shook as I applied my lip gloss. "I should have made you be the pretty one. You're better at flirting."

"Which is why I already have a boyfriend." Samantha patted off her face with paper towels and pulled her hair into a messy ponytail. Uneven strands hung out over one ear. "Come on, Juliet. You already look irresistible and the sooner we do this, the sooner we can leave."

We left the restroom and she walked toward the restaurant entrance. "Remember to slouch." I called after her. "Don't make eye contact. The world is an awful, gloomy place!"

She didn't look back at me, but several other students did. I slid back into the doorway of the bathroom so they'd all stop staring at me.

After a couple of minutes, I went into the dining room to keep track of Samantha's progress. As I stood in line to order a soda, she slunk off to the tables, looking at the floor, although this might have been because it was hard to see while wearing someone else's glasses. She held out one hand as though perpetually ready to catch herself.

No one paid attention to her as she walked over to a chair. A few people noticed her as she misjudged the distance of the chair and stumbled onto it. Even more people noticed as she grabbed her shin and did this sort of hopping step while repeating, "Youch!"

But no guys walked up, so it was all good.

Finally she took her seat.

A few tables over, Molly shook her head. Polly just squinted in Samantha's direction.

Samantha kept leaning down with her face nearly pressed against the table as she rubbed her shin. It was not an attractive look.

Good strategy. I was wrong to ever doubt Samantha's abilities to look like a loser.

The guy at the counter gave me my soda. I took a deep breath, held my shoulders erect, and strolled across the dining room. I put a bounce in my step as I walked to an empty table. Smiling at anyone in the vicinity, I sat down, and leaned back in my chair.

My heart was beating too fast. Would people be able to sense that?

The table felt colder, looked bigger than I'd expected. And emptier too. A minute passed. No one even noticed me as they walked by. Another minute wound around my watch.

It was a stupid experiment, I realized, because I had forgotten the cardinal rule of the pick up. Guys never tried to pick you up when you wanted them to. No, when you were between boyfriends and desperate, they stayed away from you like you were wearing man repellent. It was when you didn't want it and weren't expecting it that they popped up to flirt with you.

Which meant despite all our manipulations, Samantha would get the guy, Molly and Polly wouldn't get makeovers, and Mr. Metzerol wouldn't think I was helping them. Rick would win the audition, and I'd have to explain to half the senior class why I was shunning them. Then again, after Rick won the audition spot maybe everyone would naturally shun me.

See, things always work out somehow.

"Hey."

I'd been so busy brooding I hadn't noticed anyone approaching. Now I looked up and saw a guy, and not just any guy—the Clark Kent guy.

Chapter 9

He wore faded jeans and a sweatshirt, but somehow managed to look even better than he had at Rick's party.

I blinked in surprise and struggled to find my voice. "Oh, hi."

He sat down in the chair next to me and smiled but his eyes had an edge to them. "You know, when some girls run out on a guy at a dance, they at least leave a glass slipper behind to help him out. You disappeared without so much as telling me your shoe size."

I laughed, and blushed, and felt happy despite the accusation in his voice. He had the most gorgeously familiar eyes, and he had cared that I left the dance. "Sorry about that," I said. "You see, there was this thing . . ."

He nodded with his eyebrows raised. "This thing? Are you sure you don't just make a habit of fleeing from dances?"

"No, you see . . ." But I didn't want to explain any of it. How did I go about telling a stranger that Rick and his deadbeat band hated me and had written a whole CD of awful songs in my honor? "It's a long story," I said.

"I see." More nodding. "Does it involve a carriage that turned into a pumpkin at midnight?"

"No." It did involve a wicked sister, but I wouldn't go into that either.

"Then, can you tell me your name?"

I hesitated, wondering if he had listened to, or remembered the song Rick had been singing when I left. I hoped not. "It's Chelsea."

"Chelsea?" he repeated, perhaps because I'd been hesitant to answer.

I was about to ask him what his name was, when Molly and Polly walked up. Well, Molly walked up, Polly sort of shuffled over and bumped into the table. Then she put one hand down on the top to stop it from wobbling.

Right on cue Molly said, "Hey Juliet, are you ready to go to English? We'd better hurry or we'll be late."

"Juliet?" The guy asked.

"Oh, my name isn't really Juliet." I looked back and forth between Molly and Polly. "You don't have to call me that. I know this guy. He's . . ." and that's when I realized I still didn't know. "Um, what's your name?" I asked him.

He leaned back in his chair and folded his arms. "Romeo Montague."

Polly waved her hand nervously in my direction. "Come on, Juliet. We've got to leave for English. Remember— Professor Dotti and our eyebrows?"

Molly just shook her head at me, tsking under her breath. "You're pitiful. You didn't even last two minutes."

I turned back to Romeo/whoever he was. "This is all just a big misunderstanding. You see, I came here to try to pick up guys—well, no, wait, that doesn't sound right. You see, actually I wasn't really trying to pick up guys, which is why I gave out a fake name, only I didn't give *you* a fake name because I really am Chelsea."

He nodded, his arms still folded. I could tell by his expression that he thought I was insane. Which is when I knew there was no point trying to explain because I couldn't talk my way out of this situation and come out looking like a normal person. I stood up and pushed away from my chair. "Um, I'd better get going or I'll be late for English. See you around."

"Yeah, see you, Juliet."

ᔕ ᔕ ᔕ

We were able to get Molly and Polly an appointment in the salon. Dotti cut their hair shoulder length, adding layers and highlights. Then she did the eyebrow waxes. And yes, Molly shrieked during the process. Polly did one eyebrow and tried to chicken out and not do the other. We had to convince her that she couldn't walk around with uneven eyebrows.

Then we went shopping, and I found them some nice shirts that didn't cost a whole lot—which was a feat of willpower, considering I just wanted to sulk the entire time.

I couldn't believe I had met the guy again. He had looked even better than I remembered, and now he thought I was crazy. How could I fix that?

Samantha kept gushing about how wonderful the twins

looked, and even they seemed happy with the end results, eyebrows and all. I could barely manage to get out a few compliments though. My thoughts kept returning to the guy.

I knew where he worked. If I went to the Hilltop, say on a daily basis, sooner or later he'd have to be my waiter, right? And once he was my waiter I could . . . well, I wasn't sure what I could do. Maybe give him a certified doctor's note swearing to my sanity along with a really big tip.

I was as pitiful as Molly had said. I'd spoken about three sentences to him and was willing to spend my entire college fund hanging out at a restaurant. And all this for a guy who most likely wouldn't take another look at me once he learned I was only a senior in high school.

When Samantha dropped me off at my house, I paused before shutting the car door and asked her, "So . . . do you want to go out to dinner at the Hilltop tomorrow night?"

∽ ∽ ∽

Molly and Polly made quite the entrance when they walked into school in the morning. A lot of girls told them how nice they looked. The guys were silent on the matter, but even this was a good thing. No one called them Roly and Poly. I did hear the term Holy and Moly floating around, but I figured that was a compliment.

Polly smiled a lot, and told me her parents agreed to buy her contacts. Molly pointedly told me there was no way she was wearing contacts and seemed suspicious about the attention she received. But despite all of my coaching, when I saw them in the hallways between classes, both girls still shuffled their feet and kept their eyes downcast. "Watch your posture," I'd whisper to them as we passed. "You're confident, remember?"

When that didn't produce results, I took Mr. Metzerol's methods to heart and threatened to smack them in the back if they didn't straighten up. Instead of listening to me, I think they just avoided me in the halls.

At lunchtime Mr. Metzerol complimented me on their appearance though. "You're a miracle worker," he said. Of course, that was the last nice thing I heard him say. I sang my song for him again, and judging from his dour facial expression I hadn't improved since yesterday.

I got another lecture on using my diaphragm. He also told me my notes were breathy and in my throat as opposed to in my forehead, where I should be feeling them. Really. He told me that. I was supposed to feel the notes in my forehead. Which is why artistic people are so annoying, because they say these sorts of things and expect the rest of us to know what they're talking about.

Still I thanked him, promised to do my scales, my exercises, and to try and produce sound emanating from the region of my eyebrows.

After school we had cheerleading practice. Or at least we were supposed to—what we really did was practice our song. We had to do some sort of cheer routine for the halftime of the next game, but instead of coming up with a new routine, we decided to just modify our "Shoop Shoop" song and dance. Rachel, Aubrie, and Samantha would do the backup part wearing football uniforms, and I'd change the words of the song so they described a winning football team.

Easy enough and we wouldn't have to learn new dance moves.

After rehearsal I had just enough time to get home, do my homework, my chores—and all right, I admit it—primp nervously in front of a mirror before I drove to the Hilltop.

Samantha and Logan were meeting me there. Samantha because she'd been the one standing within three feet of me when I rashly decided to track down 'the guy,' and Logan because they'd barely spent any time together recently. Samantha used to work at the bookstore with Logan but had quit when school started up so she could spend more time on her studies. And she did study more—well, when she wasn't moping around because she didn't see Logan at work anymore. Anyway, Samantha insisted Logan come too because the Hilltop was "their restaurant." They went there on their first date.

I asked Aubrie and Rachel if they could come too, but they already had study plans with some guys from the team—something that Rachel sighed repeatedly about. "Can't you go to the Hilltop another day?" she asked. "Samantha already got to watch you make a fool of yourself this week."

Rachel has so much faith in me.

Anyway, it was just Samantha, Logan, and me. For once I was glad they were so engrossed in each other, because that way Logan didn't harass me about the pathetic depths my love life had reached. Although as we walked into the restaurant he did say, "Have you tried the guys at Taco Time? I bet they'd be cheaper to stalk."

I ignored him and we walked up to the hostess. Samantha and I had this part of the night perfectly planned.

"Table for three?" the hostess asked. She didn't look much older than us, definitely a college girl.

"Yes," Samantha said, "and if it's possible we'd like the same waiter we had last time."

"What's his name?" the hostess asked.

Samantha snapped her fingers and put on a look of consternation as though the name had escaped her. She turned to me. "What *was* his name?"

I shook my head. "I've forgotten, but he had brown hair, blue eyes. He was tall . . ."

The hostess considered this. "Was he an older guy with glasses?"

"No. He was young . . . and he had a nice smile . . ." I hoped the hostess would produce a name but instead she shook her head like she too was stumped. "Donald and David are both blond. Randy has red hair. John and Cleave have brown hair but brown eyes . . . Are you sure it was this restaurant?"

It had been this restaurant, but either he wasn't a waiter here or the hostess had forgotten him. And since she was a female and he was a hot guy I doubted she would forget him. So who was he? My hopes fell. "Maybe not," I said, and then I let her lead us to a table.

Dinner consisted of me glancing around the restaurant

half a dozen times just to make sure I hadn't somehow over-looked the guy, and me feigning interest in the salt and pepper shakers so I didn't feel like a third wheel in Logan and Samantha's conversation.

Maybe he worked here as a busboy or a chef. Only there wasn't a way for me to casually ask about him now that I'd told the hostess he was a waiter.

Besides, Rachel was right. The whole thing was a stupid idea. It wouldn't have worked anyway.

I ate slowly, mostly because I had no appetite. Samantha and Logan finished way before I did and then had to sit there and watch me pick at my food. "You don't have to wait for me," I told them. "If you need to go, I understand."

"We can wait," Samantha said. "It's no problem."

"Are you done with your calculus homework yet?" Logan asked her. Logan is Samantha's self-appointed tutor ever since last year when she bombed the SATs.

"Not really," she said and looked at me to see whether I wanted her to stay or not.

"You might as well go," I said. "We came in separate cars anyway."

The waitress brought our checks, and Logan took care of their bill.

"Sorry Romeo didn't show up," Samantha whispered to me.

Logan leaned closer to me and said, "Don't feel bad. It wouldn't have worked out—I've read the story and you both die in the end."

Then Samantha and Logan said their good-byes to me and walked out of the restaurant holding hands.

I dug my wallet out of my purse, laid twenty dollars on the bill, and took a drink, waiting for the waitress to come.

When she did, she looked over her shoulder, then back at me. "Can I see some ID with that?"

I blinked up at her, wondering if she'd automatically assumed I laid down a credit card. "I need an ID to pay with cash?"

"The manager requested it."

"The manager," I repeated, and blushed.

I dug my driver's license out of my wallet and gave it to her. Maybe in some horrible twist of fate I'd unknowingly given them a counterfeit bill and I'd be dragged off to a police station for questioning. Rachel would be so disappointed to have missed it.

Or maybe, yes—it was the guy, and he was walking toward me with my ID. I wondered when he had noticed me and why I hadn't seen him.

He sat down on the chair across from me and handed me both my money and my driver's license.

"I'm comping your meal, Chelsea. It was worth it just to find out what your name really is."

"Thanks." I slipped my ID back into my wallet. "I told you all along my name was Chelsea."

"Yes, but you did it under suspicious circumstances. Why was everyone else calling you Juliet?"

I hesitated, thought about it, and took the fifth. "I could explain, but I'd rather appear mysterious. Is it working?"

He tilted his head down and laughed. The tenseness left his eyes. "I guess so." He held out his hand to shake mine. "I'm Tanner. Now we've officially met."

I shook his hand, afraid I was blushing again. College girls probably didn't blush when they met guys. "Aren't you kind of young to be a manager here?" I asked and held my breath, hoping he didn't answer with something like, "Yeah, everyone tells me I look so young. Actually I'm twenty-five . . ."

Instead he shrugged. "I'm really an assistant manager. For a while my brother took to shortening the term 'assistant' to—well, it's just easier to say manager—so that's what most of the employees call me." He shrugged and his blue eyes crinkled around the corners as though he was letting me in on a secret. "My parents own the restaurant."

How come every time I saw him he looked better than the time before? "That must be nice," I said. "I bet you always get really good dinners and stuff." I didn't know what else to say and realized my last sentence had verged on babbling. Having a hot guy sitting so close will do that to you.

"I eat well when I work here," he said. "I can't say the same for dorm food."

He probably needed to get back to work doing whatever it was assistant managers did, but I didn't want him to leave. We stared at each other for another moment and then because I couldn't think of a casual way to say it, I just blurted out, "So Tanner, we didn't really get off to the greatest start. Do you believe in second chances?" The next moment stretched out as I waited for his answer.

He smiled, nodded and leaned closer to me. "Yeah, I guess I do."

"Great," I said and then mentally added as though it were a mantra, *Don't ask me how old I am. Don't ask me how old I am.*

He shrugged. "Would you like to get together sometime?"

"Sure." *Don't ask me which dorm I live in. Don't ask me which dorm I live in.*

"Can I have your phone number?"

I gave him my cell phone number. He wrote it on the back of my bill, studied me for another moment, then shook his head. "I keep trying to figure out where I know you from. Do you take Economics 101?"

"No." *Don't ask me what my major is. Don't ask me what my major is.*

"Have you ever lived in California?"

"Nope."

"Do you go to the Rec Center to run track?"

"Maybe you just recognize me from the restaurant. I come here a lot." I didn't, but I didn't want him to keep asking about my schedule.

He nodded uncertainly. "That could be it." Then his expression changed, and I could tell he'd put the matter out of his mind. "I'm closing tonight, but we could get together after classes tomorrow. What time are you done?"

"Two-thirty." Which was, after all true, because that's when the high school got out.

He nodded. "Let's get together for dinner. Can I pick you up at six?"

If I gave him my house address he'd know I wasn't a college student. My throat felt dry. "I have some errands to run tomorrow. Why don't I meet you somewhere. Where did you want to go?"

He said, "Let's go someplace where my coworkers and family won't be around. How about Basilios?"

We worked out the last of the details and then he glanced around the room. "I'd better get back to work. If I stay here too long the other employees will never let me hear the end of it." He stood up but gave me another smile before he left. "I'm glad you came in tonight, Chelsea."

So was I. All the way home I repeated his name in my mind.

☙ ☙ ☙

My friends and I generally got together on Jock's Landing before school to talk. The subject the next morning was my secret double life as a college student.

"I never told him I went to WSU," I pointed out. "I just never said I didn't."

"It's almost the same as lying," Samantha said.

"It's not lying," I said. "It's verbal camouflage."

"Camouflaged or not, he's going to be mad if you're not up front about it from the beginning," Samantha said.

Aubrie nodded. "He'll wonder what else you haven't been honest about. Besides, it's not such a big deal. A lot of the guys we dated last year are in college this year. Girls date guys who are older. People know that."

"But there's a difference between a college guy dating a

girl he went out with in high school and a college guy hitting on some random high school girl." I folded my arms and stared out at the river of students making their way to the lockers. "He'll think I'm too young for him."

"He'll find out eventually," Samantha said. "You can't hide it forever."

"I don't have to hide it forever," I said. "Just until next year when I actually go to college." Or until he decided he liked me so much he didn't care I was seventeen—well, almost eighteen.

"Why not let her pretend to be older?" Rachel asked, finally chiming in on the subject. "Chances are she'll get tired of him before he figures out her age." Rachel forgets that the rest of us don't date as much as she does.

"And how is she going to keep her age from him?" Samantha asked.

"Easy," Rachel said. "Just keep him talking about himself. That's what guys like to do anyway."

"Maybe," Aubrie said, "but the subject will come up sooner or later."

Rachel shook her head and then stared at the ceiling in contemplation. "I probably shouldn't reveal my dating secrets. Once I do, you're likely to steal all sorts of guys away from me." She lowered her gaze with a sigh. "Still, what are friends for? Chelsea needs help and she's not getting any good advice from the rest of you." Rachel took hold of my arm and pulled me closer to her. "I have a method. It works every time, and it will work for you if you can manage to follow it."

"What is it?" I asked.

"No matter what the topic of conversation is, you keep asking him questions about himself. Act like you want to talk about nothing but his thoughts, interests, and friends. If he mentions the sky is blue, you ask what he thinks about that and when he first noticed it. Don't say a word about yourself, and he'll worship you by the end of the date."

We all stared at her for a moment. Then Aubrie said, "Don't guys think it's strange that you never say anything about yourself?"

Rachel tilted her chin down. "Like they even notice. All the guys I date think I'm the best conversationalist in the world."

"Wow," Samantha said slowly. "I'm not sure if that's incredibly brilliant or horribly manipulative."

"Don't you get tired of just talking about the guy?" Aubrie asked.

Rachel shrugged. "Sure. That's where kissing comes in handy."

"I'll try it," I said.

Samantha rolled her eyes, and Aubrie shook her head sadly, but Rachel gave me the thumbs-up sign.

Chapter 10

The school day went by, haltingly slow at some times and breakneck fast at others, depending on whether I was excited or dreading my date with Tanner. Mr. Metzerol didn't hit me quite as much with his stick during my lesson with him, which I figured was progress. Molly and Polly were still slouching around, which wasn't.

Whenever I walked by him, Rick gave me dirty looks and mumbled things I knew I didn't want to hear. Rachel told me she'd heard through the grapevine that he thought I was responsible for Adrian breaking up with him. Which was typical Rick. I don't suppose it ever occurred to him that he had anything to do with it.

I knew Adrian would take him back in a second if he apologized—not even to me—just to her, but I wasn't about to suggest it. As far as I was concerned, his relationship with her could fade away, destined to be remembered with the same fondness as dental work.

I'd help her find someone new. Someone nice. Just as soon as she started speaking to me again. See, when you come right down to it, I'm much more forgiving of her than she is of me.

I changed my clothes three times and my hair twice before I went off to meet Tanner. Mom hadn't come home from work yet, so I left her a note and hoped she didn't call me on my cell phone with objections.

Tanner was already at the restaurant when I got there, and keeping with the trend, he looked even better than last time.

He smiled when he saw me walk up. "Hi again."

"Hi." Underneath the glow of his smile, I couldn't remember Rachel's instructions. In fact, I couldn't remember anything, like what to say next.

He didn't seem to notice though, and he made small talk while the hostess seated us at our table. Probably he was used to girls being speechless around him.

Dinner went surprisingly well. Mostly we stayed on safe topics—like our hobbies—we both loved skiing, and we made a date to go the first weekend after the lifts opened. We also talked about a lot of current events. I felt myself stretching to explain my opinions and the logic I'd used to reach them. He listened, and although he didn't agree with me about everything, he respected what I said. I could tell he was smart, and he made me feel like I was smart too.

When had Mike ever made me feel that way?

A few times the subject matter wandered dangerously close to identifying me as a high school senior. That's when I remembered Rachel's advice. When he asked what classes I had, I said, "Just the usual stuff. What about you? What's your favorite class?"

It was biology, something that slightly bothered him since

he'd already decided to go the MBA route. It was his family's way of life. They ran businesses.

After that we talked about business, family expectations, and whether it was wise to strike out in new directions if other things interested you.

When we finished dinner we wandered over to Baskin-Robbins for milk shakes. Not because we were hungry; neither of us wanted to say good night yet. The night air chilled my face as we walked, a reminder that November was here, and snow wouldn't be far behind. We took our cups and strolled over to the patio area near the river. The Palouse River is actually more of a stream as it runs through Pullman, and it mostly consists of mud, but it was nice to sit on a bench and look at it, because I was alone with Tanner.

He asked me where I lived—a definite danger area. If I told him, "With my family" he'd ask why. I hesitated and said, "Your parents run the Hilltop, so they must be residents. Do you live with them or on campus?"

True to Rachel's advice, he didn't seem to notice I hadn't answered his question. He said, "I'm in Perham Hall."

"Didn't want to live with your parents?"

"Didn't want to live with my brother."

"Oh, you don't get along?"

He shrugged. "Some of the time we do, but most of the time I want to kill him." He paused for a moment. "You probably think I'm terrible for saying that, don't you?"

"No. I have a little sister, remember?"

"Oh yeah." He shot me a smile. "Tell me about your sister."

Danger area. I smiled back at him. "Tell me about your brother."

He leaned back on his hands, considering. "My brother is the smartest person I know, but he's devoted his entire life to slacking off. I can't tell you the last time he helped out at the restaurant."

I nodded. "My sister blames me for all her problems."

Tanner held out his hand as though showing me something. "My brother hates everything I do. I did sports, so he won't. I got good grades, so he won't. If I've done anything, it isn't cool."

I took a sip of my shake. "My sister refuses to think about her future, plus most of the time she dresses like the bride of Satan."

"My parents would never let me get away with half the stuff my brother gets away with."

"Exactly," I said, relieved that he understood—and surprised that I'd found someone who felt like I did. "My mother is too busy dealing with my sister to pay attention to my life."

Tanner nodded and turned back to me. "It sounds like they'd make quite a pair. Maybe we should get them together."

I shook my head and fast. "No way. My sister just broke up with her loser boyfriend. I'm hoping next time she'll choose someone who wants to reform her."

Tanner shrugged. "Yeah, and actually my brother already has a loser girlfriend." He gave me a quirky smile. "She drives my parents crazy. All you have to do is say the word 'grandkids' and my mom shudders."

I raised my cup in a toast. "Here's to our future family reunions. May the normal people outnumber the hoodlums and slackers."

Tanner tapped his cup into mine. "We can always hope."

We both took a drink, but the next moment my relief gave way to sadness. Adrian and I had been so close when we were younger. Would it ever be that way again?

I looked down into my cup and didn't say anything. I felt Tanner's gaze on me, but he didn't say anything either. Maybe he understood my silence just like he'd understood my complaints.

Finally I looked back up at him. "I really love her," I said. "I worry about her all the time."

He put his hand on my back and rubbed a slow pattern of consolation across the material of my jacket. "I know what you mean."

He kept rubbing my back and I leaned my head into the crook of his shoulder. How had this happened so fast? Usually on a first date I worried about what kind of impression I made. I'd not only told Tanner about Adrian, I'd leaned into his shoulder like I'd known him forever.

Neither of us said anything for a moment. Then Tanner said, "I'm sure you're a really good sister."

I straightened up to tell him he was wrong. There were many times when I was an awful sister, but before I could say anything he leaned over and kissed me. Which put thoughts of Adrian right out of my mind.

It's not that I hadn't been kissed before. But kissing Tanner made me feel like it was the first time. My heart pounded and I felt dizzy and happy and awkward all at the same time.

When he finally stopped kissing me, I didn't know what to say and felt myself blush bright red. That's the problem with blushing. Telling yourself that you shouldn't do it, doesn't help at all.

Tanner smiled at me then looked away. I could tell he was weighing some matter in his mind, trying to decide something. At last he said, "My grandmother is coming from California for a visit in a few days. We're having a big family dinner up at the house on Monday. I know it might seem too soon to meet my family but it would be nice to have you there, you know, to kind of balance out my brother's loser girlfriend and show Grandma that one of us has normal taste. Do you want to come?"

"Sure." That's how much I liked Tanner. I wanted to spend time with him even if it meant meeting his family, his slacker brother, and a loser girlfriend.

கு கு கு

I spent the rest of the week working on homework, singing practice, and dance rehearsal. We had it down perfectly, and it looked good. Sometimes while we ran through it, I imagined myself performing under a spotlight that illuminated me to thousands of screaming fans. What would it feel like to be a star? To be rich? To be famous?

Even though I tried to be realistic and not get my hopes

up, thoughts would pop into my mind. I'd look across our cramped kitchen and think, "If I had a music deal, I could buy my mother a new house."

Unfortunately this thought was quickly followed by, "If my dad found out I was rich, he would try to take the money from me."

I spent about half an hour one night worrying about this, and remembering the times when I was little and he emptied my piggy bank because he needed money for liquor. My father wasn't nice when he was sober, but he was worse when he was drunk. I didn't have a good childhood.

Most of my early years were spent watching out for Adrian because she was a couple of years behind me in understanding how to keep out of his way. We either roamed around the neighborhood like miniature nomads on bikes, or we hid in my room, inventing fairy spells to keep him away. Our best one was touching the doorknob, then tapping the edge of the door three times when we passed by.

Even after Dad moved out, Adrian kept doing the spell for years. She said it worked on keeping all sorts of bad things away, and I admit I did it periodically for insurance that he wouldn't come back.

You would think the courts wouldn't have given my father joint custody of us, but they did. So we're all just glad he lives far away and never visits. Once in a while he calls, mostly to complain how my mother has ruined his life, and how he can't pay child support, but we can live with that.

If I came into any money before I turned eighteen though, could he get a hold of it?

This caused me actual anxiety until I realized my father wasn't likely to even call before I turned eighteen let alone find out my financial status, so I had nothing to worry about. I let myself return to the daydream of being discovered, of hearing myself on the radio, of Mr. Metzerol just once nodding proudly and telling me my potential was officially shaped.

In real life, Mr. Metzerol continued to prod and poke me through my voice lessons. He told me that Molly and Polly still refused to sing solo. He said this like I could change their minds. Right. I couldn't even get them to agree to come to the movies with a few people from school, and believe me, I tried.

Samantha and I invited Aubrie, Rachel, and half the football team—including Joe—to go to the movies with us on Friday. Molly and Polly wouldn't come though, because in English class Polly heard Joe say he was going bowling. Yes, bowling. I was trying to play Cupid and the boy would rather flatten a bunch of bowling pins.

Mike and Naomi, of course, showed up. This hardly bothered me though, because while we stood in line to buy tickets, Tanner text messaged me twice from work. He complained that the weekends were the busiest time for restaurants and tried to entice me to stop in by telling me the specials. *The lobster is fresh*, he wrote. Like I needed lobster to persuade me to see him. If I hadn't been stuck in line, he could have lured me in with dry toast and pretzels.

I must have been smiling a lot because while I texted him back, a couple of the guys commented on what a good mood I was in.

"It's the new boyfriend," Rachel told them. "Chelsea's seeing a college man."

They both went "Ohhhh," like it explained everything.

"It's not that," I said. "It's just that life is a wonderful, precious gift so we should be happy."

Both of the guys laughed and one said, "Yeah, she's got it bad."

The other imitated my voice and said, "Life is a precious gift. Well, my life, anyway. Your life ain't worth squat because you ain't got my boyfriend."

And they laughed some more. Out of the corner of my eye I noticed Mike. He wasn't laughing. In fact he glared over at us, but I didn't care.

On Saturday and Sunday I doubled my singing practice, but I still couldn't get notes to properly come out of my forehead. I followed Mr. Metzerol's instructions. I went around for an hour doing diaphragm exercises and practicing scales. Once when I got to the point where I sang, "Mi-mi-mi-mi-mi-mi-mi-ii" Adrian strolled by and shook her head. "Isn't that the truth?"

Instead of getting Adrian in trouble for this kind of commentary, Mom bent over backward to be nice to her. On Sunday when Adrian skipped out on helping with the dinner dishes and disappeared into her room—an impenetrable fortress of screeching guitar music—instead of calling her to come out and help, Mom just did Adrian's job for her.

"She's having a hard time right now," Mom told me as she cleared off the table. "We can be sensitive about that."

"No one was sensitive to me when Mike dumped me."

"But you've dated lots of boys," Mom said. "We knew you'd find someone else quickly. And you have. Don't you have a date tomorrow?"

Well yes, but there had still been several weeks that I had sworn off men altogether and no one had done the dishes for me.

"Adrian dumped Rick, not the other way around," I said. "I don't see why she's so upset about it."

Mom poured uneaten green beans into a container and put them on a shelf in the fridge, where we would undoubtedly ignore them until they went bad. "Why don't you try to talk to her about it?"

After I finished loading the dishwasher, I went up to Adrian's room. She was sprawled out on her bed painting her toenails black, intent on ignoring me. I walked over to her CD player, turned down the music so she could hear me, and in my most sensitive voice, I asked her how she was doing. Then I gave her the "There-are-other-fish-in-the sea" pep talk, followed by the "I'll-help-you-go-fishing" pep talk.

She looked at me in stony silence for a moment then said, "First of all, you don't understand anything about Rick. Second, you don't understand how I feel. You've never lost anyone you've cared about because you don't really care about guys. They're all just one more picture to make your myspace look like you've got an online hot-guy fan club. Mike, by the way, was a total flake."

And Rick wasn't? This was a little like the Corn Flakes insulting the Wheaties.

"Third," Adrian said, "I wouldn't trust you where guys

are concerned, anyway. You'd set me up with someone and then decide you wanted him yourself."

That stung, but I should have expected it. It was the one card Adrian pulled out any time she wanted to trump whatever I said and show me what a horrible person I was.

You see, there was this thing about a year ago. . . . No, it's been longer than that. It happened during the end of my sophomore year; it just seems more recent because the memory hasn't faded.

When had Adrian started to like Travis Woods? I couldn't remember. Sometime in elementary school. She used to watch out our living room window for him every morning so we could time our walk to school with his. I thought it was cute, sweet, even if I didn't know what she saw in him. To me, Travis was just another slightly annoying boy in my class.

It wasn't like Adrian sat around pining for him when he didn't notice her. By seventh grade she had rotating crushes. But even then Travis was always in the background of her thoughts. He grew six inches and filled out into a good-looking guy, which goes to show you that Adrian has an eye for potential. I didn't blame her anymore for liking him. A lot of girls liked him.

When she came to see all of the freshman football games, I knew it wasn't to watch me cheer. Her eyes were glued on number 96. When we ran into each other in the neighborhood, she always complimented him on whatever pass, tackle, or interception he'd made. He thanked her with this quirky smile, like he didn't deserve the hero worship, but appreciated it anyway.

The next year when I put together that sophomore biology study group, I did it with Adrian in mind. Travis would be there. Granted, I knew nothing would happen between them. I mean, let's face it, no self-respecting sophomore guy hits on an eighth-grade girl, but we were laying the groundwork for her freshman year, just a few short months away.

During every study group, Adrian hung around, finding ways to linger near Travis. Often she lingered too long and said stupid things. I tried to coach her on the delicate balance between letting a guy know you're interested and trapping him on the couch with stories of your PE flag football adventures, but she wouldn't listen to me. Apparently I no longer knew what I was talking about. In her mind she had already made the jump to high school, and she didn't need me to navigate her course.

I could see Travis mentally labeling her as an annoyance, a groupie. He pulled away from her, cut her out of the conversation. The harder I tried to convince Adrian to ease up, the harder she tried to get his attention. She actually asked him about his summer schedule and then tried to invite herself to some of his activities.

Which was pretty much the kiss of death. She'd killed her chances and didn't even know it.

After our last study group ended, Travis left, then came back five minutes later. He'd forgotten his notes. Adrian had gone to her room and I was in the middle of cleaning up soda cans and half-empty bowls of popcorn. He picked up his notes then helped me take dishes into the kitchen.

We'd left a few things out in the living room, but I felt bad making him clean. "I can get the rest," I said.

"No, I'll get it," he said, then paused a foot away from me. "Is Adrian around?"

I sent him an apologetic smile. "She's in her room. You're safe."

He laughed, the kind of laughter which is actually gratitude that someone understands. "She's a nice girl and everything, but . . ."

"I know. She comes on a little too strong."

He stepped closer to me and spoke softly, to make sure our voices didn't carry. "I don't want to hurt her feelings, but I don't know what to say to her. Isn't there someone her own age she's interested in?"

"Yes," I said even though it was a lie. I didn't want to make my sister sound like a stalker. "She likes a couple of guys in her class, it's just that when you're around she can't help but flirt with you. Consider it a compliment. You're irresistible."

He laughed again, and I noticed how his eyes lit up when he smiled. His sandy blond hair was mussed up in a way that made you want to run your hands through it. "Yeah," he said without an ounce of belief in his tone. "I wish I had that effect on women."

"You do. In fact, I bet you have entire eighth-grade blogs dedicated to the twinkles in your eyes."

He took another step closer to me. I should have turned away from him then, but I didn't. I stayed there, leaning against my kitchen counter smiling at him. This is how it's done, I wanted to tell Adrian. See how easy it is? I still know more about flirting with guys than you do.

He looked down at me mischievously. "If only women my own age felt that way about me."

"Who says they don't?"

He bent down slowly. I could have moved away, but instead I closed my eyes and let him kiss me.

It only lasted a minute. Just long enough for the thrill of being right to wear off. With his lips still on mine, I thought, *What am I going to do now? How am I going to explain this to Adrian?* But I knew I wouldn't explain. I'd hide it and never let her know what I'd done.

And then I heard Adrian gasp. I pushed away from Travis and saw her standing in the kitchen entryway. Her mouth hung open in shock and her eyes looked wide and frightened. Frightened, not hurt. I didn't understand that back then, but I think I do now.

Fear is what you feel when the person who's always protected you slices through your heart. The world is no longer a safe place; it's one where anyone can turn on you.

Adrian spun around and dashed back to her room, leaving a wake of silence in the kitchen. Travis ran his hand through his hair. "I'm sorry. I guess I'd better go."

He departed almost as quickly as Adrian had, and then I was left standing there with a horrible, empty feeling pounding in my chest.

I tried to talk to Adrian. I apologized to her over and over. I told her I'd never see Travis again. It didn't matter. I didn't have any good reasons for what I'd done, and saying, "It just happened," was perhaps worse in the end.

"It just happened" became Adrian's new excuse for everything. Her tongue piercing just happened. Her grades dropping just happened. Her black wardrobe just happened.

Every time she said it, she told me everything was my fault. And from that day forward she reconstructed herself into someone who was the exact opposite of me.

Now looking at Adrian painting her nails with sullen resolve, it hurt all over again. I let out a sigh. "How long are you going to bring up Travis for?"

She turned from her toenails to her fingernails. While I watched she gave herself long, black claws. "Just until I get even."

I didn't say anything else to her. There wasn't a point. Some people will never forgive you. It's too much fun hating you instead.

Chapter 11

On Monday Samantha, Molly, Polly, and I spent all of history class working on our report. It was nearly done. This was not my fault. I'm not one of those people who plan to leave things to the last minute, it just happens naturally. The last minute works for me.

But Molly and Polly would have none of it. They wanted to get the project done right away so we wouldn't have to worry about it later. I tried to point out that it was just as easy not to worry about it now and then worry about it quickly later. In fact, it was probably more worry-effective because really, how much can you worry about something at the last minute?

Polly said, "Look, we know you're busy with your cheerleading and practicing for those auditions and all. We can take care of typing the report and doing the bibliography if you don't have time for it."

Which was touching considering they'd started out the project insisting that they weren't going to let me cheat off of them. Still, I didn't want to make them do most of the work, because I hadn't been nice to them so I could slack off. I'd been nice to them so that Mr. Metzerol would give me voice lessons.

Which sounded just as bad, but it wasn't. I mean, I liked Molly and Polly. That had to count for something.

So then I had to tell them, that no, I didn't want them doing my work for me, which meant I had to try and plow through it quickly so I didn't let everyone else down.

Although really, Samantha was having a hard time concentrating on her part: Space travel, the early years, because she was mad at Logan.

When she'd met Aubrie, Rachel, and me at our usual chat spot that morning, she crossed her arms and shook her head. "It happened again."

"What happened again?" Aubrie asked, already sympathetic.

"Logan drove me to school this morning, and I used Rachel's method and asked him questions about his interests." She held up one hand to emphasize her point. "He talked about himself all the way to school."

We stared at her waiting for more information, which didn't come. "Well, wasn't that the point?" Aubrie asked.

"I've been doing it for three days. It's been three days that I've said nothing about myself, and he hasn't even noticed. Or cared. I could be a computer program that repeats, 'What do you think about that, Logan?' and he'd be just as happy with me. Apparently my contribution to our conversations has always just been to take up dead space until he could talk about himself again."

Rachel shook her head. "I told you it gets boring if you do it non-stop. Remember, that's what kissing is for."

Samantha tossed her hair from her shoulder. "I don't want to kiss someone who doesn't care what I think about anything."

Aubrie looked at each one of us in turn, her expression growing stern. "See, I told you that whole-just-make-him-talk-about-himself thing was a bad idea, but no, you wouldn't listen."

"Actually," I said, "it's worked out great for me."

"Kissing," Rachel said as though making a point.

Samantha grit her teeth. "I was sure by this morning he'd get suspicious. I mean, if he wouldn't talk about himself, I'd think he was hiding something. I'd start questioning him about it. He doesn't even care that I could be keeping things from him." She flung her hand in my direction. "I could be living a secret double life like Chelsea."

"And I'm happy being a college student. College guys are more mature."

Samantha let out a sigh. "Maybe I should become a college student too."

∽ ∽ ∽

Between space flight, and trying to hold onto notes with my diaphragm so Mr. Metzerol wouldn't jab me with his stick, I hardly had time to think about Tanner until he called me that afternoon. He wanted to know where he should pick me up for the dinner at his house.

Yeah, I should have figured that out beforehand, since I didn't want to tell him that I lived with my family. "I'm going to be at the library working on a project," I said. "Why don't you meet me out front?"

This still wasn't lying because I could work on the space flight stuff up at the campus library as easily as anywhere else. It just meant I had to take the bus up there to do it.

The whole double-life thing could get complicated if I didn't confess everything soon. I mean, there is a fine line between verbal camouflage and out right lying. Tonight, I decided, after our date, assuming it went well, I'd tell him the truth.

Tanner picked me up at six o'clock and we drove to Sunnyside Hill. He tapped his finger against the steering wheel as he drove. "I probably should warn you that my grandma is opinionated. She's old and rich and thinks that gives her the right to say anything she wants."

"Oh," I said, "I'll remember that."

More tapping. "My brother, of course, is also opinionated. He's young and rebellious so he thinks that gives him the right to say anything he wants."

"I understand," I said.

"Richard's supposed to be on his best behavior tonight, but that's not saying much. Grandma thinks he should go to Juilliard and he's trying to get out of it."

It only vaguely registered that this was the first time Tanner had told me his brother's name. I dredged my memory for everything I knew about Juilliard. It was an exclusive music school in New York. Very hard to get into. My next-door neighbor had practiced hours each day on the piano trying to get in and hadn't made it.

"Your brother plays the piano?" I asked.

"Juilliard isn't just for pianists. It has other programs. Grandma thinks if Richard wants a future in music, Juilliard is the place to go. She has connections so she thinks she can get him in." Tanner grunted and shook his head. "My brother's last comment on the subject was that he'd rather eat a classical guitar than play one." He glanced at me with an apologetic smile. "I'm only telling you this so you'll know what's going on if they start in on each other."

It seemed like an odd thing to argue about. "Isn't it his choice where he goes to school?"

"Sure. And Grandma can choose to do something else with his trust-fund money." Tanner shrugged. "You see how it is. Richard wants to be independent, but not so independent that he has to support himself on a musician's salary."

We stopped at a large brick home with an immaculate yard. Tanner opened the car door for me, which was so nice. Not only did he treat me like I was smart, he treated me like I was a lady.

When we walked into the house, Tanner's mother was the first to greet us. She gave Tanner a hug and me a big hello. She told me to call her Barb and said I was welcome over any time. Then Tanner's dad came up and shook my hand. They seemed so happy to meet me that I liked them immediately, and not just because I noticed Tanner's dad give him the thumbs-up sign while I was talking to his mom.

Then Tanner and I walked into the living room to meet *The Grandmother*. I knew, from the tone Tanner had used to describe her, that she wasn't a "nanna" or any other endearing terms grandchildren use. She was *The Grandmother*, said in the same tone one would say *The Godfather*.

As soon as I walked into the room I saw her perched in a Queen Anne chair. She wore a dark skirt, a blazer, and a pearl set that made me feel underdressed in my jeans and sweater. She lowered a china teacup and peered at me with bright, dark eyes, like a bird surveying its surroundings.

"You must be Tanner's girlfriend." Her voice was more welcoming than I'd expected. "Come here and let me have a look at you."

Tanner and I both walked over to where she sat. Her gaze followed me, appraising me like I was something to be bought.

"Very pretty," she said. "You're a student?"

"Yes, Ma'am." I'd never said the word "Ma'am" before in my life, but it somehow popped out, extracted by her presence.

"Do you get good grades?"

"I try." Probably not hard enough to impress her, but I wasn't about to admit that.

Tanner leaned toward me, brushing his hand against mine. "Grandma, you're meeting Chelsea, not hiring her for a job."

The Grandmother raised a hand and swatted away his objections as though shooing a fly. Without taking her eyes off me she asked, "And what field are you going into?"

"I haven't decided. I like fashion design."

This apparently was the wrong thing to say. She cocked her head and made a disgruntled coughing sound. "Oh, you're one of those girls who spend all day shopping at the mall."

"No," I said, "but there are so many girls who do, fashion designers will always be in demand."

The Grandmother laughed, conceding the point. "That's the type of thinking that makes money, at least if you know your area of expertise. Tell me, if I wanted to dress down this skirt what would I wear it with?"

Tanner said, "Grandma—" but I held up my hand to stop his protest. I knew the answer to this question.

"You could trade out the blazer for a twin set or a ruffled blouse. Something that doesn't button up to the neck. You'd also want to replace the pearls with a silver chain."

"Not gold?"

"Your skin tone looks better with cool colors."

"What brand of clothing would you suggest? Escada? Dolce & Gabbana?"

"The designer labels are nice, but you can find stuff that's just as well made for way cheaper."

The Grandmother smiled at me and nodded in Tanner's direction. "She's talented and thrifty. Keep ahold of her. She's going places." She lifted her tea cup again, signaling my interview was over. She took a sip, then raised her voice slightly and called, "Why don't you follow your brother's example, Richard, and find yourself a nice girl like this?"

I hadn't realized that anyone else was in the room and now I turned in the direction she was looking.

Lying down on the couch so that he blended in with the throw pillows was Rick.

Chapter 12

*R*ick? Richard was *Rick*? Tanner was Rick's *brother*?

Rick sat up; his eyes focused on me angrily. "There's a thought," he called back. "Are there any more at home like you, Chelsea?"

It didn't seem possible that this was happening, and yet it was. Rick was here. Tanner had never told me his last name. Apparently it was Debrock.

Rick looked different than usual. He had none of his earrings or eyebrow studs in. He wore an unremarkable pair of jeans and a T-shirt. Even his hair was almost a normal shade of blond. Too bleached, but within the shades of actual hair color.

"Rick." It was all I could say, and I barely managed that. The word came out half strangled.

"It's Richard," The Grandmother said. "He was named after my husband and my husband always went by Richard." She took another sip from her cup. "Nicknames are so vulgar."

Rick rolled his eyes, but didn't seem interested in fighting this point.

I tried to keep my voice even, unaffected. To Tanner I said, "You didn't tell me Rick—Richard—was your brother."

"Didn't I?" He looked genuinely surprised by this fact. "I thought you knew the night we met at his party, but then you left so quickly, maybe it never came up."

"I did leave quickly," I said, glancing at Rick.

Rick shrugged, "Well, my music isn't for everybody."

I didn't know what to say, didn't know how much of our relationship to divulge. Would Rick tell his brother and grandmother that I was the one who'd inspired his anti-cheerleader songs? Should I?

The Grandmother took another sip of her drink and looked at me. "You don't like Richard's music?"

I didn't hesitate. "No, I've never considered electric guitar to be real music. Classical guitar, now that's a different story."

It was perhaps an underhanded thing to do, but Rick deserved it. And it had the immediate desired effect. The Grandmother nodded and put down her cup. "You see, Richard, it isn't because I'm old. There is simply a difference between good music and bad—between melody and discordance— between depth of voice and that awful stuff you insist on singing." She waved a hand in my direction. "Even young people can see it."

I smiled over at Rick. He glared back at me. "So you like classical guitar, Chelsea? And who exactly are your favorite classical guitarists?"

I didn't have to answer because The Grandmother wasn't through with her remarks. She went on and on about how if

Rick wanted a career in music he ought to take it seriously enough to become trained.

Tanner and I sat down on the couch across from Rick, and Tanner sent me apologetic looks because his grandmother was delivering this huge lecture.

I enjoyed it though. I nodded along to every point she made.

When The Grandmother finally paused long enough for Rick to get a word in he said, "Yeah, all that's great, but Juilliard doesn't train people to sing rock. Just opera."

"Exactly," The Grandmother said. "Rock isn't serious music."

Rick glanced at me and paused. I could almost see him mentally rearranging his argument to incorporate the strategy I'd used. "But rock music sells. You don't see people packing into stadiums every weekend to hear operas."

The Grandmother drew her brows together, factoring this new aspect into the discussion. After all, one did have to take money into account. Then she shook her head. "But most rock musicians will never succeed. They'll spend their lives wasting away, playing bars and free outdoor concerts. If you went to Juilliard you would at least have something to fall back on. You could teach music."

I thought of Rick with a mustache and tie like Mr. Metzerol's. It made me smile.

Rick leaned forward, his hands lifted, and his expression intent. For once, he actually cared about what he was saying, and I felt for him. Momentarily I rooted for him to win this argument. "Look Grandma, if you could just hear my band—"

She folded her hands across her lap. "You gave me the Deadbeats CD. I haven't been able to get farther than halfway into the first song."

"No, if you could only see me sing and watch how people react to my music. My band can make it. It's going to take some time; it always does. But we'd be able to pay you back for the equipment and give you a good return on your investment."

So there was more to it than just a difference of opinion about classic guitar. Rick wanted his grandmother to help finance his band.

"Come watch the *High School Idol* auditions," Rick said. "You'll see then."

The mention of *High School Idol* immediately and firmly removed any sympathy I felt for Rick. He would sing about me. He wanted his grandmother to help his band succeed and then the whole world could listen to horrible Chelsea songs.

Rick had been, and still was, the enemy.

"I suppose I could come," The Grandmother said. "But I doubt it will change my mind. Juilliard is the best thing for you."

Rick grunted and leaned back into his couch.

I smiled over at him. "I hear New York is beautiful in the fall."

Tanner's mom popped into the room. "We're all ready. Let's eat."

We sat down at the dining room table, complete with tablecloth and china. At my house we didn't have a dining room or china and I couldn't shake the fear that I would do something wrong.

This feeling wasn't helped at all by the fact that Rick sat sullenly across the table from me. It was just a matter of time before he said something to let his family know that he went to school with me and that he didn't like me. Both of which would make dinner really awkward.

I should have told Tanner how old I was before, but there was nothing I could do about it now. It was one more mistake to add to my long list.

I hoped Tanner didn't act too shocked or too disappointed or say something along the lines of, "You knew I thought you were in college. Why didn't you tell me the truth?"

Was there any way out of this? I didn't want to lose Tanner, and I didn't want to be humiliated in front of Rick.

I ate dinner and smiled and made small talk, all the while feeling stiff, waiting for Rick to blow my cover. Every once in a while I felt his gaze on me, thick with resentment, but he didn't say anything. I guess Tanner was right; Rick really was on his best behavior for his grandmother.

Tanner's mom smiled over at me. "We hardly know anything about you, Chelsea. Why don't you tell us about yourself?"

"I um . . ." What could I say that wouldn't reveal anything about myself? I couldn't even make something up because Rick would know I was lying and call me on it. I glanced over at him. He was watching me. "I've lived in Pullman my whole life," I said and then hurriedly added, "I understand you moved here from California. Do you find Pullman very different?"

"I miss all the sunshine," Mrs. Debrock said.

"I don't miss the crowds though," Mr. Debrock added. "Or the California housing prices."

"I miss the people the most." Rick gazed back in my direction. "The kids at school are all jerks."

I gripped my water glass and didn't answer.

"Rick had to move here during the end of his sophomore year," Mrs. Debrock explained. "He's had a hard time adjusting."

I smiled sympathetically. What else could I do?

"Tanner stayed with me in California to finish high school," The Grandmother said. "Because he was a star player on the lacrosse team, and Pullman High doesn't have lacrosse." She leaned toward Tanner, the pride evident in her face. "Did you tell Chelsea you're in the lacrosse club?"

Tanner glanced at me and smiled. "It never came up in conversation."

"He's quite modest about himself," The Grandmother said. "In California, his team was first in the state. He's a natural talent."

"I'm impressed," I said.

Tanner shrugged off the compliments, like it embarrassed him to have his abilities dragged out and presented at the dinner table. Rick rolled his eyes.

So that's how it was. Tanner was the family's golden boy, the favorite child. It made me feel sorry for Rick, which wasn't a welcome sensation. I didn't want to think of Rick with friendly parents, a critical grandmother, and china at dinnertime. It changed everything and yet it changed nothing. Rick still periodically glared at me like I'd sneaked uninvited into his house. He'd probably incorporate this night into his next song about me. It would be called "Invasion of the Cheerleader."

I put on my best poker face and tried to answer his glares with a confident posture. *Go ahead and tell them why you hate me,* I tried to say with the tilt of my head. *It will only make you look bad in front of your brother, your parents, and the woman you want to finance your band.*

But just in case he flunked posture reading, I also put Rachel's advice into full swing. I wouldn't give Rick time to talk. I asked about Tanner's sports accomplishments. I asked about the Hilltop and whether it was hard to run a restaurant. I asked The Grandmother how she'd learned about business, and that topic took us all the way through dessert.

Tanner's grandmother had graduated with honors from college back when most women didn't even go. She'd taken one restaurant and turned it into a successful chain that spanned three states. She'd invested in real estate. She had a wide range of friends in the business world. I found it all fascinating, mostly because it had nothing to do with me.

By the time I was done with my raspberry-drizzled chocolate cake, I not only wanted to tell Rachel she was brilliant but to declare her a dating goddess. She had saved me. Tanner didn't know the truth about me, and his parents and Grandmother adored me.

I might actually be able to tell Tanner about myself in the car on the way home instead of around the dining room table with everyone gasping at me.

After we'd finished with dessert, I asked, "Would you like

help with the dishes, Mrs. Debrock?" I figured this was better than sitting around the table chatting.

She looked over at me, genuinely surprised. "That's sweet of you to offer, but you're our guest. Besides, I don't want to take you away from Tanner."

"He can help too," I said. It had never been my plan to leave him alone with Rick.

I glanced over at Tanner to see if he minded being volunteered, but he was already on his feet, picking up plates from the table. "It's fine, Mom. You should relax. You and Dad made dinner."

Tanner headed to the kitchen with his hands full of dishes, and I followed after him, holding several plates. Right before Tanner left the dining room, he looked over his shoulder and said, "Come on, Richard. You grab the glasses."

I held my breath, waiting for Rick to come up with an excuse not to help. After all, the boy was a professional slacker. How hard could it be for him to come up with some place he needed to immediately be?

"Sure," he called back to us. "I'd love to help." And perhaps only I noticed the sarcasm.

In a preemptive conversational strike, I told Tanner how nice his family was while I rinsed dishes off. Tanner took the plates from my hands and stacked them in the dishwasher, agreeing. Rick went back and forth from the dining room to the kitchen bringing us dishes and silverware.

At one point Tanner took the linen napkins to the laundry room and Rick and I were left alone. He dropped the rest of his silverware into the tray and then surveyed me with a nod. "Nice way to kiss up to everyone. You are truly a master to watch."

I smiled at him and leaned against the counter top. "Are those future lyrics?"

"I write it as I see it."

"Maybe you need to take a better look around then."

He shook his head, still surveying me. "I can't believe you're dating my brother." He gazed off in the distance, raised one hand then dropped it. "Maybe I should have seen it coming. Maybe your type just naturally finds each other, like sharks in mating season." His gaze returned to me and he waved a finger in my direction. "But don't think you're going to start hanging out here now, because you're not."

As if I wanted to spend more time around Rick. "You didn't seem to mind intruding at my house whenever you felt like it."

He took a step toward me. "Well, you pretty much took care of that, didn't you?"

"No, *you* did. You're the one who wouldn't apologize."

He rolled his eyes. "Oh. Okay then. I'm sorry."

"Are you still going to sing 'Dangerously Blonde' for *High School Idol*?"

"Yeah," he said. Only he used several adjectives too. Well, at least I think they're adjectives. I've never actually diagrammed a sentence with swear words in it so I'm not sure.

I smiled back at Rick. "Maybe if your grandmother won't finance your band, she'll want to finance mine. After all, she thinks I'm going places."

He took another step closer to me. "I can think of a few places where you could go."

"And the only place you're going is Juilliard. Have fun learning classical guitar."

Rick took one more step, but I never found out what he was going to say because Tanner walked back in. He looked at the two of us and I saw him note how close Rick stood to me. A flash of annoyance crossed Tanner's features and he came and stood on the other side of me. Possessively near.

Did he actually think that Rick was putting the moves on me? It was almost funny. Tanner spoke to his brother, and his voice had an edge to it. "Did you bring in all the silverware?"

Rick didn't move away from me. "Yeah."

"Why don't you go check and make sure you got it all."

"Because I know I got it all."

"Then take the tablecloth to the laundry room."

"Who made you kitchen dictator?" Rick asked, but he turned and stalked out of the room.

Once he was gone, Tanner looked at me questioningly, perhaps still trying to figure out what had happened between Rick and me. I knew I couldn't wait any longer. It had to be right now. "Um Tanner, I have something to tell you. A confession really. I should have told you before but I liked you, and I really wanted you to like me too."

His expression clouded and I knew he was expecting me to say something horrible.

"I'm only seventeen. I don't turn eighteen until April."

His expression remained clouded, like he was still waiting

for the horrible part. When I didn't say anything else he said, "Right. You're seventeen. I saw that on your driver's license."

"You knew? All along you knew I wasn't in college?"

His eyes widened. "You're not in college?"

"No, I'm only a senior in high school."

"Oh—I thought you'd skipped a grade or something. You're still in high school?" I couldn't judge how bad he considered this to be, because immediately recognition filled his features. "You know Richard from school, don't you?"

"Yeah, although we're not . . . friends." I said this because I was stalling, because I still didn't want to come right out and tell him we were enemies. It was more than I wanted to discuss right now, but since I knew Rick would say things about me after I left. I added, "I guess I should warn you that he doesn't like me."

"Really?" I didn't imagine it, relief drained into Tanner's expression. "Sorry about that. But don't take it personally. He doesn't like most people. He doesn't like me."

He said this so cheerfully that I laughed. And it was nice not to have worry about the truth exploding on me anymore. Still, it didn't mean that Tanner would overlook this turn of events. I took a deep breath. "Does it bother you that I'm so much younger than you?"

Tanner stepped closer to me and took a hold of one of my hands. "You're not that much younger. I'm only a freshman. I'm eighteen."

How could that be? "But Rick is a senior—"

"Richard skipped a grade and we're two years apart." Tanner took my other hand and smiled as though an idea had just occurred to him. "You know, if I'd moved here with the rest of my family, I would have gone to PHS, and we probably would have dated."

I leaned closer to him. "Then we're just making up for lost time."

"Right." He bent down to kiss me. His lips had just touched mine when Rick came back in.

"Oh great," Rick said. "My kitchen is no longer safe to walk into."

Tanner stepped away and smiled at me apologetically. "Don't mind Richard. He's just in a bad mood because his girlfriend didn't come tonight." Then to Rick he said, "Where is she anyway?"

Rick brought his Grandmother's teacup to the dishwasher and put it in. As he did, he glanced at me. "She broke up with me."

"Really?" Tanner's voice was surprised, and then turned sympathetic. "When did that happen?"

"A while ago. Her older sister didn't think I was good enough for her."

I came so close to saying, "And her older sister was right," but I bit down on my lip instead. I didn't want to appear petty and vicious in front of Tanner. I just glared back at Rick instead.

"You're kidding," Tanner said. "Adrian let her older sister dictate who she went out with?"

"Apparently," Rick said.

Not true. And I would explain the whole thing to Tanner once Rick wasn't standing there glaring at me.

"Well it's a good thing you found out now what kind of girl she is. Otherwise you'd have to remake yourself every time she didn't like something."

This about a guy who thought his hair color should match his outfit.

Rick leaned up against the counter and looked down at the floor sadly. "Yeah, I know. But it still sucks."

Tanner shook his head and a hard edge crept into his voice. "And what kind of judgmental shrew says you're not good enough for Adrian? I'll tell you what; Adrian wasn't good enough for you."

Rick didn't look up. "Nah, I always knew Adrian out-classed me."

"Only in detention appearances," Tanner said. "Come on, if Adrian hadn't worn so much hairspray her head would have flown off long ago. Forget about her—no, I take that back; remember that she was nothing but white trash in black leather. She probably only saw you in terms of dollar signs and a nice ride. You're better off without her." It was only then that Tanner turned to me. "Don't you think Rick could do better?"

"No," I said. "Actually I don't." And I had to ungrit my teeth to get that much out.

That's when Rick started laughing.

I stepped away from Tanner. "Look, thanks for dinner, but I think you should take me home now."

Tanner looked from me to Rick and back again. "What's going on?"

Rick held his hand up, his thumb and finger almost

touching. "Buddy, you were this close to having that trophy girlfriend you always wanted."

"What are you talking about?" Tanner asked.

Rick shook his head, still enjoying himself more than he should have. "Apparently Chels never got around to telling you, but Adrian is her little sister."

Chapter 13

The ride home was painful, but thankfully short.

Tanner apologized as he walked me to the car, but I barely heard it. His words had sliced into me and I didn't even want to look at him.

After we drove for a few moments in silence, Tanner said, "Really, I'm sorry, but you should have told me."

"I would have, but I couldn't find a way to casually fit that in between the judgmental-shrew remark and the hairspray comment."

He gripped the steering wheel harder than was necessary. "I was just trying to make my brother feel better after a breakup. Can't you understand that? How was I supposed to know Adrian was your sister?" Then he shook his head and let out a groan. "I should have figured it out. That's why you looked so familiar. Your smile, your voice, your mannerisms— you reminded me of Adrian."

I folded my arms tightly across my chest. "The girl you think is a gold-digging idiot? Am I supposed to feel complimented or insulted by the resemblance?"

"It's not an insult—I just—oh, nothing I say now is going to be right, is it?"

I looked out the window. "Do you know the way to my house? We, of course, live in the white trash part of town."

He didn't answer but drove in the general direction of my neighborhood so I didn't give him more directions.

"You know, it's not like you've been praising Richard," Tanner said. "Last Tuesday you told me your sister broke up with her loser boyfriend. That was my brother you were talking about."

"Yeah, and he deserved the title. Your brother is a jerk. Adrian is just . . . misguided."

"Misguided?" Tanner let out a cough. "You're the one who said she dresses like the bride of Satan."

"And I'm allowed to say that because she's my sister. But I never said she was stupid, or white trash, because she's not. Oh, and also I'm not a judgmental shrew. I didn't break Adrian and Rick up. That was your jerk-of-a-brother's fault."

"My-jerk-of-a-brother? So you're allowed to insult Richard, but I can't say anything bad about Adrian?"

"You can insult Adrian right after she writes horrible songs about you and sings them to everyone you know."

His eyebrows drew together. He had no idea what I was talking about. It was very possible that he'd never actually listened to any of the words of Rick's songs.

"Just ask him why I think he's a jerk. Eventually he'll get to the right answer."

We approached Jefferson Elementary School and Tanner

slowed down. With his jaw clenched tightly he said, "I know you live around here, but I don't know which street."

I gave him directions, calmly, all the time wishing that we lived in a house half as nice as his. He pulled up in front of our small one story, and I noticed that our bushes were overgrown again and a pair of Adrian's muddy tennis shoes lay scattered across the front porch. She was supposed to have taken care of those days ago.

Tanner put the car in park and turned to me. His blue eyes flashed with anger and I suddenly realized who he reminded me of. Rick. I'd seen that look on his face a hundred times. "Hey, I'm sorry I called you a judgmental shrew," he said, "when clearly you're not judgmental at all."

I flung open the car door and stepped outside. "No problem. And by the way, Adrian *is* too good for Rick." I slammed the door and stomped across the lawn to my front door.

Once I got inside I noticed Adrian sprawled out on the couch by the living room window. "Was that Tanner Debrock's car?" she asked.

I walked past her without answering. Then I went into my room, leaned against the door, and cried.

છ છ છ

I drove to PHS the next day. Usually I walk because it's only fifteen minutes away, but I wanted to get to school early to talk to my friends. I needed to talk to someone and Adrian, sitting beside me in the car with her MP3 player blaring and her eyes shut, was not a good candidate.

I hooked up with my friends at our usual meeting place and told them all about my dinner at the Debrocks'. There was a lot of gasping and Aubrie held onto my arm and made a several, "Oh . . . oh no . . . oh *noooo!*" comments.

Rachel shook her head slowly. "What are the chances of you meeting up with Rick's older brother?"

"I guess I increased my odds by going to two places where Rick's band was playing, but really, who would have guessed Rick had such a normal and good-looking brother?"

Aubrie joined in the head shaking. We probably looked like a row of cheerleading bobble head dolls. "It's so ironic. If you hadn't made Adrian break up with Rick, then Tanner wouldn't have said those things about Adrian—and you and Tanner would still be together. This is just like one of those Greek tragedies."

"I didn't make Adrian break up with Rick," I said. "So it isn't ironic, it's just Rick's fault." I'd never made the connection Aubrie had, and it immediately bothered me. I was already in a lousy mood, and this only made things worse.

Samantha folded her arms. "I'm with Chelsea on this one. She's better off without Tanner. Guys will break your hearts if you let them. That's just what they do."

Which I supposed meant she was still upset with Logan.

Aubrie patted me on the shoulder. "At least this way you won't have to worry about getting Rick as a brother-in-law. I mean, wouldn't that have been ironic—just as you get rid of Rick in your sister's life, you pick him up in your relationship with Tanner?"

Yeah, ironic, apparently no matter what I did my life was doomed.

Aubrie gave a shudder and her eyes grew distant as though contemplating a new truth. "It's almost like you and Rick are destined to be together somehow."

"Never say those words to me again," I said.

"Don't worry about it," Rachel said with a shrug. "Once you win the auditions you'll have your pick of hot Hollywood guys. Rick and Tanner will be a distant memory."

But I couldn't imagine it. I couldn't imagine Tanner's face fading into the recesses of my mind. I would probably never see him again, and just the thought of that hurt.

Logan found me as I walked to my first class. He strode up next to me as I navigated my way through the hallways and with barely a "Hi Chelsea" for a greeting, said, "So, do you know why Samantha is mad at me?"

"Yeah. But it's not a big deal. She just followed Rachel's dating advice and it backfired on her."

He cast me a confused glance. "What?"

I realized too late that I shouldn't have mentioned Rachel or her techniques. She would not appreciate it if the guys at PHS got wind of her methods. It was better to let them all think that yes, she really was fascinated by everything they had to say.

"Look, you just need to ask Samantha some questions about herself," I told Logan. "That's all she wants."

"What?"

I held my hand out to him as though this would help with the explanation. "She's mad at you because even though she's been asking you nonstop questions about yourself, she still wants to talk about herself once in a while."

Now his eyebrows drew together in consternation. "*What?*"

"Logan, why do you keep saying that?"

"Because women make no sense." He put one hand on his chest. "She's mad at me because she wants to talk about herself? Does she need my permission to do that? Why has she been asking all those questions about me if she wanted to talk about herself?"

"Because she wants you to adore her."

Logan raked his hand across his hair. "My head is going to explode. It can only take so much illogic."

"But Samantha also wants you to care about her opinion, which is why all you need to do ask her what she thinks about a few issues. Casually. Without her knowing that you're doing it on purpose or that you talked to me about it."

Logan stared at me for a moment and then looked off into space, shaking his head. "It's amazing we've survived as a species. Truly amazing."

"Oh, like guys make sense."

"Guys make perfect sense," Logan said. "But you need a degree in psychology to understand women."

No, you didn't. You just needed to talk to their friends every once in a while—thus ensuring the survival of the species. I might have pointed this out but we had to go our separate ways in the hallway so I just yelled out, "Good luck."

In history class Samantha was in a better mood. I supposed this meant that Logan had accomplished his mission.

But I didn't ask because my mood had gotten worse as the day went on. At my voice lessons Mr. Metzerol told me I breathed too much. How can a person breathe too much?

When I walked by Jock's Landing, Mike and a bunch of the other football players were all laughing about something. As I got near they suddenly stopped and watched me in silence.

So subtle. Like I couldn't tell they were talking about me. I would have rather heard what they said because now I just conjured up all sorts of ugly things.

Sure there were still people who were nice to me, and my friends tried to cheer me up and tell me it would all blow over, but it only takes a couple of mean people to make you feel awful.

In history class Molly and Polly told me to look on the bright side. There were only 216 more days of school left until we graduated. They'd kept a running total since they moved in. They used to have calculations for the hours, minutes, and seconds too, but had lost track of those since their makeovers. I considered this a good sign. To their credit, each girl had kept up with her hair, makeup, and wardrobe improvements. Or as Molly put it, "Now it takes me forever to get ready for school."

Polly told me that she was picking up her contacts after school, and that she'd started jogging in the evening. "Maybe if I slim down, Joe will talk to me."

"Or maybe he'd talk to you if you talked to him first," I said. But no, she didn't want to try that.

After school, as I took books out of my locker, Rick

strolled up. He wore mirrored sunglasses and a gangster-looking trench coat.

"Hey Chelsea, I just came by to tell you sorry for dinner last night."

I glanced at him suspiciously. "What are you sorry for?"

He gazed away from me, like he was too cool to make eye contact. "Whatever you want. Tanner told me to apologize and I said I would. So now I have."

He turned as though leaving, but I didn't want him to go. Just hearing Tanner's name made me want to pull more information out of Rick. "Hey, apologies don't count if you don't say what you're sorry for."

He tilted his head and grunted at me. It was then that I noticed a red mark running along Rick's cheek and disappearing under his glasses. "Is something wrong with your eye?" I asked.

"No." He leaned away from me, obviously hiding something.

"Yes, there is." I reached up and snatched the glasses off his face. A red welt surrounded by a bruise went from the corner of his eye to his cheek bone.

I let out a gasp. "Did Tanner hit you?"

Rick grabbed the sunglasses out of my hand and put them back on his face. "No, Tanner didn't hit me. It was the ceiling fan."

"The ceiling fan hit you?"

"Yes."

"You were bothering the ceiling fan's girlfriend too?"

Rick scowled to let me know I wasn't funny. "I was standing on top of the coffee table to get my car keys off the entertainment center and the ceiling fan hit me."

Which still didn't make sense. I leaned against my locker and surveyed him. "Your car keys were on top of the entertainment center?"

"Yeah, Tanner threw them up there after I chucked them at him."

"Why did you chuck your car keys at Tanner?"

Even behind his sunglasses I could see Rick roll his eyes. "Use your imagination, Chels. We were fighting. Do you need to ask what we fought about or are you pretty clear on that?"

I wanted to think that Rick was mad at Tanner for insulting Adrian, but I wasn't sure. "What?" I asked.

Rick shook his head and laughed at me. "You're the kind of girl that likes it when two guys fight over you. Well, I'm sure it wasn't the first time for you, was it?"

Uh, what planet was he living on? When had guys ever made it a habit of fighting about me? It's not like there was a line forming to ask me out or anything. Especially since his stupid "Dangerously Blonde" had become the school's unofficial theme song.

Rick took a step toward me so he was nearly touching my locker, and lowered his voice. "This is your way of spreading more joy in my life, isn't it? It's not enough that you made Adrian break up with me, you had to make my brother hate me and my grandmother insist that I play the classical guitar."

Which was really too much. "I didn't do any of that," I

said. "You did." I slammed my locker door, hard. So hard that it bounced back open and hit Rick right in the face.

His glasses flew off, now in two pieces. He staggered backwards, groaned, and put his hand over his eye.

"Oh no," I said, and then, "I'm so sorry!"

He kept his hand pressed over his face. "Sure you are."

"You don't think I did that on purpose?" I stepped over to him, trying to check for bleeding or swelling. "Are you all right?"

He didn't move his hand away from his eye. "I'm probably blind now."

"Let me see it."

"I don't want you to see it."

"Stop being a baby, Rick. Let me just check to see if you're hurt."

With one eye he glared at me. "I'm pretty sure I can tell on my own if I'm hurt. It got me right where the ceiling fan did."

I pried his hand away from his face and held onto it with my own while I peered at his wound. It did look worse, more swollen, and his eye was red and watering. "Can you see me?" I asked.

"Adrian," he said.

Which meant it was bad if he couldn't even tell who was standing in front of—wait a minute. I spun around and saw my sister, her hand on her hip, staring at us.

Her eyes narrowed, and she shook her head disdainfully. "I can't believe you." Then she spun around and stalked off down the hall.

Rick pulled his hand away from mine like my touch burned. "Thanks," he spat out, and trotted down the hall after her. I watched him catch up to her. He tried to speak to her, but she hurried on, not looking at him.

Yeah, this was all going to translate into another great evening at home.

I walked slowly out to my car, and even waited for her, but Adrian never showed up.

Chapter 14

When Mom came home at 5:30 Adrian still hadn't appeared. I had to tell Mom what happened. She looked at me skeptically after I'd finished the story. "Were you flirting with Rick?"

"No," I said. "I don't usually do that by smashing my locker door into a guy's face."

"But it looked like you were flirting?"

"Well, maybe if you consider me examining a guy's facial wounds while he's crying flirtatious . . ."

"But you stood close together and held his hand," Mom accused.

"I was checking his vision. I said, 'Can you see me?' Those aren't words of endearment or anything."

Mom tapped her fingers against the counter and looked off in the distance. "Adrian might have thought you meant, 'Can you see me' as in 'Let's start seeing each other.'"

What? I threw up both hands. "Why would I want to see Rick? She knows Rick and I don't like each other. It's been months since Rick and I said two civil words to each other."

Mom turned back and stared at me, her gaze accusing again. She didn't say anything else.

"Don't bring that up," I said. "This isn't the same."

Mom turned her gaze from me to the phone. "I'll try her cell phone again."

I'd already tried it a dozen times, but I didn't argue.

When I'd finished up the dinner dishes and Adrian still hadn't come home, new waves of worry spread over me. What was she doing? Why was she so mad? Certainly Rick had explained what happened. She had to know he wasn't lying. He had the welt to prove it.

I shouldn't be so concerned.

But I was. To look at Adrian you wouldn't think of her as fragile. Fragile people didn't wear black leather. Yet Adrian seemed to continually run along the edge of destruction, to always be putting one foot far enough over to feel the air on her toes.

I took my cell phone into my bedroom and fingered it while I paced back and forth between my bed and dresser. Finally I called Tanner. Our fight didn't seem important now, and he'd know Rick's cell phone number. Rick probably knew where she was.

Tanner answered the phone, his voice cautious. "Hi Chelsea."

"Hi Tanner." I couldn't just blurt out that I wanted Rick's phone number, and besides, hearing his voice made my heart skip in an unexpected and aching way. I decided to start at the beginning. "Rick apologized to me at school today. He said you told him to. I wanted you to know I appreciate it, even if immediately afterwards I did smack him in the face with my locker door. That was an accident. It really was."

Tanner's voice turned incredulous. "You hit him with your locker door?"

"Accidentally. And um, have you seen Rick since school? I mean, I couldn't tell how badly he was hurt. Do you have his cell phone number?"

A hint of suspicion crept into Tanner's voice. "You want my brother's number?"

"For Adrian."

"Adrian already has his number."

"No, I mean, Adrian walked up while I was checking Rick's face and she thought . . . well, I think she thought that Rick and I were doing something."

Tanner's suspicion turned to alarm. "Exactly how were you checking his face?"

I let out a sigh. Not this from Tanner too. Were Rick and I the only ones who'd noticed that we didn't get along? "I was just looking at his eye. That's all. But I had to pull his hand away from his face first, so I was sort of holding it in mine, and Adrian saw us and stomped off. She hasn't come home yet." My throat clenched and I could only get the rest out in a whisper. "I'm worried and I need to talk to her. I need to explain."

Tanner's voice turned soothing. "I can give you Richard's number. That's easy enough, but if he is with her, wouldn't he have explained everything to her?"

"I guess, but she doesn't trust me. She . . ." My voice came out in an uneven rhythm. "See, there was this thing with this other guy . . ." I didn't want to tell him. I knew he'd think less of me for it, but at the same time I wanted him to understand why Adrian acted the way she did. In halting phrases I explained about Travis.

He listened quietly and I wished I could see his face to judge his reaction, to judge how awful he considered my confession to be. What did he think of me now that he knew I'd stabbed my own sister in the back? Perhaps it was better that I couldn't see him, after all.

"I just thought you should know," I finished up, "so you'd understand why I got so mad at you yesterday. Adrian isn't white trash. She wouldn't be this way if I hadn't messed things up for her."

"She's told you that? She blames you for the state her life is in?"

"Not exactly in those words, but yeah."

He paused for a moment to let out a grunt. "That must be a power trip."

I didn't answer because I wasn't sure what he meant. Was it a power trip for me because I had the ability to mess up my sister's life or did he mean it was a power trip for her because she could lay this huge guilt trip on me?

I stood staring at my dresser but not seeing it, trying to work it out in my mind.

He spoke again, this time his voice sounded almost businesslike. "I'm sure Adrian's fine, Chelsea. I'll call Richard for you and see what I can find out, then I'll call you back."

I guess he didn't think I was coherent enough to talk to Rick right then, which was probably true.

I sat on the corner of my bed waiting for my phone to ring and thinking over what he'd said. Between Adrian and me, who had the power? Was there a balance? Where had it shifted to? Was it wrong for me to want it back again? After a few minutes the phone rang.

"I called Richard," Tanner told me. "He tried to talk to Adrian at school, but she wouldn't listen—just kept calling him a hypocrite and stormed off. He doesn't know where she is."

"Oh." The word left my throat hollow.

"Do you need help looking for her?"

I wasn't sure whether he was volunteering Rick's help or his own, and I didn't want Rick's help. "We haven't checked with her friends yet. But thanks for the offer."

"She'll be okay. She's probably just blowing off steam somewhere."

"Probably," I said.

"Look, I've got to go work right now, but I'll talk to you later, okay?"

I wanted to keep talking to him. In fact, I wanted to lean up against him like I had on our first date. But he wanted to hang up.

I tried to force some cheer into my voice. "Right. Thanks. Talk to you later."

We hung up and I walked out of my room to tell Mom that Adrian wasn't with Rick. Before I'd even shut my door, I heard Adrian come in. I could tell by the way Mom laid into her. "Where have you been? I've been calling you for the last half an hour."

Adrian answered defiantly. "I was thinking."

"Well, next time you can answer the phone while you think."

"I didn't feel like talking."

A pause and then Mom's voice softened. "Chelsea told me about school. She was just checking Rick's face. Nothing happened between them."

"She was just checking his face?" Adrian nearly spat out the words. "Is that her new excuse? I admit it's better than, 'It just happened,' but only slightly."

"You saw Rick. Chelsea said she hit him with her locker door."

"Yeah, I saw him, and yeah I believe that Chelsea hit him with her locker door." I could tell that she meant it, and I stood in the hallway shaking my head. If she believed me, then why was she so upset? I took a step toward the living room to ask her.

"But what was he doing at her locker in the first place, and since when did she start holding his hand, even in sympathy?"

"You don't really think that Chelsea is going after Rick, do you?"

I stopped, still hidden by the hallway, waiting to hear Adrian's answer. It might change if she saw me. Her answer wouldn't be the truth then, just whatever she thought would bother me the most.

"Do you know what first attracted me to Rick?" Adrian asked, bitterness lacing her voice. "He was the one guy I knew who would never choose Chelsea over me. Everyone else likes her best. Chelsea walks into a room and—poof—I become invisible. Do you know what it's like to live your life always second-best?"

"You're not second-best," Mom said. "If boys can't see that—"

"It isn't just the boys. She's pretty, she's popular, and she gets whatever she wants every time. When people find out I'm Chelsea's sister, I always get the same reaction: a look of surprise on people's faces, the look that says, 'How can you be Chelsea's sister? You're not blonde and gorgeous. What a disappointment. We wanted another Chelsea.' "

"Adrian, you're fine the way you are—"

"I don't want to be fine. I want to be noticed, and loved, and better than Chelsea at something."

I couldn't have moved if I'd wanted to. My insides felt like they'd been shredded. It's not my fault, I wanted to say. Why can't you see that none of this is my fault? How can you hate me for being pretty and popular? What did she want from me? Misery? And at the same time I understood everything she said, and I hurt for her.

The living room was quiet for a moment and I knew my mother had wrapped her arms around Adrian. "Honey, you *are* loved. Very loved."

"Chelsea could have any guy she wanted but she went after Rick. She had to prove she could take anything she wants away from me."

Mom's voice was still soothing. "You don't really think there's anything going on between Rick and Chelsea, do you?"

"Who did she go out with last night?"

Mom paused. "I don't remember his name, offhand."

This was because I'd been purposely vague about the matter. I hadn't wanted her to realize I was dating a college guy.

"Exactly," Adrian said as though offering evidence in a court. "Chelsea never told us his name, but she came home in Rick's brother's car."

"Are you sure?" Mom asked.

"I'm sure. I guess they thought I wouldn't figure it out if Rick didn't drive his jeep."

I went back into my room then. I knew Mom would momentarily be storming in to question me and I didn't want to let her know I'd eavesdropped on the whole conversation.

I sat on my bed, picked up a novel, and stared down at the pages. I couldn't have read it if I wanted to. My hands shook too badly.

It would be so easy to tell both of them the truth. I just had to explain that I'd gone out with Tanner and I would be cleared of all charges. Mom would rejoice that I hadn't stabbed my sister in the back again. Adrian would forgive me for holding Rick's hand. Everything would be fine.

For the first thirty seconds I sat there, I planned on doing just that.

But then I thought one step further. After Adrian learned the truth, she would also forgive Rick. She'd probably even apologize to him for calling him a hypocrite at school. And then they would get back together. I could see it happening as clearly as I could see the book in front of me.

I had—in effect—sent Adrian to Rick when I'd betrayed

her the first time. She said the only reason she'd chosen him was that he was the type of guy who didn't like me. So when she'd come to high school, she had just looked through the assortment of boy burn-outs in order to find someone to mend her ego.

Rick had worked, but he wasn't good for her. He didn't really love her. Rick was like my father, the kind of person who only cared about himself. If she stayed with him who knew where she'd end up.

But I could save her. And I could redeem myself from my mistake with Travis. All I had to do was keep my mouth shut and let her stay mad at Rick. Indefinitely if possible. So what if she was mad at me too? That had been the constant in our relationship for over a year.

Mom opened the door without knocking. "I need to talk to you."

I put down my book and waited. All I had to do was to hide Tanner without it looking like I was hiding Tanner.

"Adrian said you went out with Rick yesterday. Did you?"

My sister was probably somewhere nearby, listening. I waited a second to make my answer less convincing. "No."

"He didn't bring you home in his brother's car?"

"No." All the truth.

"Then why does Adrian think he did?"

I shrugged. "Because she wants to get me in trouble?"

Mom let out a sigh, but didn't contradict me. Her voice turned soft, and I knew she didn't know who to believe. "Adrian is going through a hard time right now. We need to be understanding, supportive . . ." Her voice faded off. She looked at my bedspread, then back at me. "Just promise me you won't do anything to hurt your sister, okay?"

"I won't," I said.

One day Adrian would realize what I'd done for her. One day she'd thank me.

Chapter 15

The next day Mom left for her geriatrics conference in
Arizona. She lined up Adrian and me in the kitchen in
the morning and gave us all sorts of cheery instructions about
what was in the freezer for us to eat, taking out the trash,
house rules—that sort of thing. She would be at the conference Wednesday, Thursday, and Friday then return home Saturday, but wouldn't reach Pullman until the evening, long
after my audition for *High School Idol* was over.

I couldn't blame her for missing it. She'd told me about the
conference before I decided to audition. Besides, I knew she
didn't want to go. She kept glancing at Adrian and me saying,
"You two will do your best to get along, right? No fights?"

"Right," I'd always answer.

Adrian only shrugged.

She gave us more instructions, told me she only wanted
me driving the car when I had to, and told Adrian not to drive
it at all. Adrian only had her learner's permit. Then Mom
hugged us good-bye. We walked to school without talking,
mostly because Adrian had her headphones firmly connected
to her ears and wouldn't look at me.

I spent the time thinking about Tanner. Without even trying I could conjure up his face in my mind—from his piercing blue eyes to the straight line of his jaw. He'd made Rick apologize to me. Something I'd never thought was possible.

But he was Rick's—my archenemy and sister's exboyfriend's—brother. Plus, I was trying to hide him from Adrian. The boy might as well have had "Danger! Do Not Touch!" stamped across his forehead.

I knew I couldn't see him again. I wanted to, but I couldn't. I'd have to give him up for Adrian's sake. All the way to school this thought clung to me like to cold rain from a downpour. When he called me, I would have to tell him that I couldn't see him again. I tried to think of a subtle and painless way to do this. I couldn't think of anything—anything that wouldn't be painful to me, anyway.

Then I worried whether I'd have the resolve to break it off with him when I really didn't want to. Was there a way I could see him and keep it from Adrian?

All my worrying was for nothing, though, because the entire day went by without a word from Tanner.

Thursday morning at school our topic of conversation with my friends was, "Do guys really mean it when they say they'll call you later?"

"It's only been a little while," Aubrie pointed out. "He probably just doesn't want to look too eager. He'll call."

But Aubrie is illogically optimistic, so you can't weigh her opinion too heavily.

"I think he'll call you," Samantha put in. "After all, he

took you to meet his parents. Guys don't do that unless they really like a girl."

Rachel, the dating goddess, bit her lip and didn't say anything.

"Well?" I asked her.

"You seemed needy when you called him about Adrian. Nothing scares off guys faster. A little helplessness, they like. It makes them feel macho to be bigger and stronger, but they flee from girls who are needy, depressed, or high maintenance. In fashion world terms, you gave yourself a dry-clean-only label for a wash-and-wear guy." Rachel shrugged her shoulders. "Look at it this way though: you messed up on Tanner, but think of how well prepared you'll be for the next guy."

I knew she was right. But I didn't want the next guy. I wanted Tanner with his easy smile and Clark Kent features. Throughout the day I kept checking my phone for text messages that never appeared.

It was so depressing that not even a compliment from Mr. Metzerol during my voice lessons—and I swear this was the first one he'd ever given me—could bring me out of it.

"Good tone!" he said, nodding vigorously during my song. "You're finally holding onto those notes. You can feel it in your diaphragm, can't you?"

I could feel it in my throat, where I felt all of my notes, but I nodded anyway. I'd never admitted to him that when I sang, my notes didn't wander around my body like they apparently did in his.

Still there was no doubt that my diaphragm was stronger.

In fact I'd done so many exercises it was probably the strongest muscle in my body. I bet my diaphragm could beat up other people's diaphragms. It could maybe even rip open car doors and leap over buildings.

In history class, Mrs. Addington let the class go to the library to work on our reports. We were done with ours, so Molly and Polly spent the time trying to cheer me up.

"Only 214 more days until high school is over," Polly told me brightly.

"Yeah, but then I have to go to college."

"College will be better," Molly said. "Because you're not stuck seeing the same small group of people every day."

"No, then I'll just have to worry about running into Tanner on campus." I put my arm on the table and rested my chin in my hand. "Plus the Hilltop has great food and now I'll never be able to go there again."

"Oh, you can go there again," Samantha said, "but only with really gorgeous guys."

Molly tilted her head in mock sympathy. "So that means you'll only be able to eat there, what, every other weekend?"

Why does everyone think my life is way better than it really is?

"It's not like there are gorgeous guys hovering around me," I said.

Molly grunted. "You've been through two since the start of the school year and it's only the beginning of November."

I didn't think getting dumped twice in quick succession was a good thing, but this was useless to point out. I turned to Polly, who was still in the new stages of contact wearing and had looked teary-eyed all period. "Speaking of love, how have things been going between you and Joe?"

Polly fidgeted with the edge of her paper. She blinked but I wasn't sure if it was the emotions or the contacts. "I still haven't worked up my courage to say hi yet."

"It's one word," I said. "Two letters. You don't need a lot of courage to say hi."

More fidgeting from Polly. "Easy for you to say."

"And easy for you to say too. If it doesn't look like it's going well you can turn your greeting into a cough. See, like this," I straightened up in my chair and put on my best actress face. "Hi-aaa—aaa—ack."

Samantha shook her head sadly in my direction. "Is it any wonder Chelsea is so popular?"

Molly nodded patronizingly, "When I grow up I hope I'm as cool as you."

"Why wait to grow up," I said, "when you can work on being cool right now?"

Molly shook her head and held up one hand as though warding me off. "Oh no. No more makeover stuff. I don't need any more hair ripped out of my body."

"This won't hurt," I said. "We'll work on your posture."

Molly leaned away from me. "And that doesn't hurt? You've smacked me in the back all week to work on my posture."

"We'll do something different this time. We'll walk with books on our heads."

With a little more encouragement—meaning that I had to promise I'd stop walking up behind them, yelling, 'straighten up!' and thumping them between the shoulder blades, they agreed to go behind the history section with me.

Samantha came too. She thought the exercise would be easy to do since she had good posture, but her book slipped off as often as Molly and Polly's did. Only I could walk and turn without *The World of Shakespeare* toppling off my head.

"It's your hair," Molly accused. "You've obviously used industrial strength hair-spray and the book is now glued to your head. I bet you could carry a four-course meal up there."

I did a turn like a model on a catwalk and smiled. "It's talent. Next I'm going to do a river-dance routine."

With her hands held out like she was walking a tightrope, Polly made a successful turn. "If I keep walking like this, do you think Joe will notice me?"

"Sure," Molly said taking a tentative step. "Who wouldn't notice that you're wearing *The Atlas of the Medieval World* on your head?"

Both Samantha and Polly laughed, sending their books crashing to the floor. That's when the librarian came over and kicked us out of the library.

We walked back down the hallway slowly, hoping that Mrs. Addington wouldn't notice that we'd gone AWOL. Polly tried to walk with her posture as straight as possible. "How do I look? Confident?"

"Or recovering from a back injury," Molly said.

"I think I could talk to him if the time was right," Polly said. "You know, if it wasn't the middle of class."

Samantha said, "He and Garret are having a party after the game on Friday. You should go."

Molly grunted and shook her head. "To a football party? They'd never let us in."

"They would if we came with you guys," Polly said, her gaze skipping between Samantha and me.

I hesitated for a moment. If Polly and Molly showed up and everything went well, then they'd gain confidence, maybe enough confidence to sing whatever Mr. Metzerol threw at them. But if it didn't go well, if people were rude, then they'd hate high school even more, and never listen to me again.

A risky venture at best, but what could I say? Polly wanted to go. "Sure, we can take you." I glanced over at Samantha but she was already shaking her head.

"Logan and I have a date after the game. He asked me to pick anything I wanted to do so we're watching *Pride and Prejudice* over at his house."

Molly and Polly simultaneously went, "Ohhhh. I love that movie."

Samantha smiled dreamily. "I know. Isn't Logan the greatest?"

Poor Logan, being forced into watching a chick flick. I supposed that would teach him not to go too long without asking Samantha her opinion on things.

"But go and have a good time at the party," Samantha said. "You guys can tell me all about it afterward."

"Right," I said, and made a mental note to ask Rachel and Aubrie to come with me. If all three of us brought Molly and Polly, there would be less chance of anyone being rude.

I spent the rest of the period coaching Molly and Polly

on what to wear, say, and do at the party. It turned out that neither of them had ever watched a football game before, and their lack of knowledge on the subject was truly frightening. I told them that they both had to go to the game on Friday so they'd be able to talk about it with Joe at his party.

I was so busy doing this that I didn't check my phone again until after school. That's when I saw Tanner's text message.

He'd sent one sentence: Do you still believe in second chances?

I stared at the message, trying to shore up my resolve. I had to think of Adrian. But then somehow I found myself thinking about the way Tanner had held me close and kissed me. It was a dizzying sort of experience a person couldn't just forget. I texted him back: Yes.

In the card game of life, a good kisser apparently trumps resolve.

He called then, and told me that they were having a special on prime rib at the restaurant and they'd probably have some left over. If I thought my family would use it, he'd drop it by after he finished work around ten o'clock.

This immediately presented a glitch in my plan to hide the fact that I was seeing Tanner Debrock. I couldn't very well parade Tanner around my house and not expect Adrian to notice this fact. At the same time, after our rocky start, I wanted to convince Tanner that I was as normal as possible. If he pulled up to my house and I was sitting outside on my lawn in the cold at ten o'clock waiting for him, and then didn't let him into my house, he might cross me right off the normal list.

I said, "Um . . ."

"You don't like prime rib?"

"No, it's great. It's just that I'm going to be at Samantha's house tonight."

"At ten o'clock?"

"Late-night studying. Do you mind dropping by there instead?"

He said he didn't mind, so I gave him directions, hung up with him, and then called Samantha. I explained the whole situation to her—how it was all for Adrian—and asked if I could come over.

She listened quietly, and sighed when I was done. "We're back to verbal camouflage? Aren't relationships supposed to be based on honesty?"

"Don't be ridiculous," I said. "If relationships were based on honesty, none of us would wear makeup."

"If you date Tanner for long, Adrian will find out about it. She'll put two and two together."

"Yeah, but hopefully by then Rick will have moved on to the next girl who's tragically lacking in taste and common sense."

Samantha's voice sounded patient, as though trying to show me reason. "Adrian will be mad at you for deceiving her."

"I haven't deceived her. I've told her all along that there's nothing going on between me and Rick. Is it my fault that she won't believe me?"

"Chelsea . . ."

"Can we talk about this later? Like at 9:45 at your house?"

She sighed again. "I'll see you then."

It was 10:15 when Tanner came by, which was plenty late

considering that Samantha had done nothing all night but shake her head and throw out sayings like: Honesty is the best policy, a clear conscience is a soft pillow, and all sorts of stuff about a tangled webs. When these didn't change my mind she finally said, "You're letting your sister think Rick likes you. That's just mean."

"Yeah, but the ends justify me being mean," I told her. I didn't get to say more because Tanner finally rang the doorbell. I told him Samantha and I had finished studying and did he want to go out for a bite to eat and to talk?

He stood on the doorstep, a warm silhouette against the cold night air. "We've both got school in the morning. I won't keep you up any later." He lifted the bag in his hand. "But besides the prime rib, I also brought you some cheesecake. We can eat a slice at your house if you want."

Samantha, who stood next to me in the doorway, sent me an arched-eyebrow all-of-your-plotting-was-for-nothing look.

I smiled back at Tanner. "Cheesecake sounds great, but this late at night my sister is usually wandering around the house half dressed . . . why don't we just eat in my car?"

He looked over at my Hyundai. "Let's eat in my car. It has a better heater."

I said good-bye to Samantha, all the while giving her my I-told-you-my-plotting-would-work look.

She watched Tanner and me head across the grass. "Good luck on your ethics test!" she called to me. "Remember, the ends don't justify the means."

"Ethics? Is that what you were studying?" Tanner asked.

I glanced back at Samantha, but she'd already shut the

door. "Yeah." I didn't want to have a conversation about ethics right now. Especially since Tanner would probably expect me to know all sorts of philosophical things for my imaginary test.

"Oh look, it's snowing," I said. As we walked to his car, chunky snowflakes fell on our head and shoulders. Apparently winter had decided to move in.

Tanner left the bag with the prime rib on the hood of his Accord where it would stay cold, but took a Styrofoam box and some plastic forks out so we could eat the cheesecake inside the car. I liked the fact that he'd packed plastic forks. It meant he'd thought about it and wanted to eat dessert with me tonight. Well, either that or he thought my family was too poor to afford utensils.

We climbed into his car and he turned the heater on high. I shivered for a minute, but I wasn't sure if it was from the cold or just being so near to Tanner.

At first we didn't talk much. We just said the usual sort of, "So what have you been up to?" small talk. I watched the snow glittering in the light of the street lamp and wondered if that's all he'd say. But when we were nearly done eating, Tanner's face grew serious and I knew he was getting ready to say whatever it was that he'd come to say. He leaned against his door so he nearly faced me. Slowly, as though he'd given it a lot of thought, he said, "I've told myself since Monday night that things would never work out between us so I ought to forget about you."

I shrugged as though hearing this didn't bother me. "Oh? How's that going?"

With an almost accusing look, he shook his head. "Not so well. It turns out you're hard to forget." He waved his fork absentmindedly in my direction. "It's probably your eyes. Did you know they're the exact same color as the ocean at Oahu?"

"I've never been to Oahu."

"You'll have to trust me about that then." He took a bite of cheesecake and considered me for a moment. "It could also be your smile. When you smile you look like you have all these secrets you're about to share, like you'll let me in on some inside joke because you think I'm special."

"Oh." I didn't plan on smiling then. It just happened.

"We seem to smile a lot around each other," he said. "Have you noticed that?"

I nodded.

Tanner gazed up at the ceiling of the car. "Of course maybe it's just impossible to forget you because Richard brings you up every five minutes."

I stiffened. "Rick talks about me?"

"Oh yeah. Mostly along the lines of: How can you like the girl who wants to ruin my life? Or, Mom, talk some sense into Tanner. He can't date Chelsea. She tried to kill me."

The fork went limp in my hand. "He told your mother I tried to kill him?"

"Yeah, death by locker door." Tanner sent me a reassuring smile. "Don't worry, Mom didn't believe him. Very few people are actually killed by locker doors." Tanner's warm blue eyes rested on mine and his voice softened. "Besides, my parents like you."

"Your parents have good taste."

"So do I. I have good taste." His gaze turned intense then, and my insides warmed by degrees. "I want to keep seeing you, but I'm not sure how to work this out. Do we try to reach a truce with our siblings? Do we ignore them and pretend we're both only children? Or maybe we should lie to each other—I'll say I think your sister is sweet and you can tell me my brother is charming."

"Let me try that." I put my fork to my mouth, gently tapping it against my lower lip. "I think Rick is charming."

Tanner nodded, his lips slightly twitching. "And Adrian is a sweet girl."

I pointed my fork in his direction. "I can tell you're lying."

Tanner dipped his chin down and laughed. "Well, you said 'charming' like it was an insult."

"Yeah, and let me tell you Rick is the prince of charming."

Tanner took my fork, put it with his into the empty Styrofoam container, and set it in the backseat. "Okay. Maybe we just need to agree that we'll both do our best to be nice to each other's siblings and never talk about them again. We can't change them, and we don't want to spend our time together discussing them anyway."

"Right," I said. "And actually now that you mention it, I think it would be best if we didn't hang out at my house. Since Adrian broke up with Rick, well, I just don't think she needs any reminders of him."

"That's fine," he said, and sounded relieved that I didn't want to force him into spending time with Adrian.

So much for honesty being the best policy. I was getting an A+ on this ethics test.

"We can go other places. I'm not working Saturday."
Tanner moved closer to me. With his arm stretched across the
back of the seat, he played with the ends of my hair. I shivered again and this time it was definitely not from the cold.

"Good."

I knew he was about to kiss me and then the subject
would be gone forever, so before he did I said, "Tanner, did
you know your brother is singing a song about me for the
auditions?"

He leaned closer to me, his hands twining through my
hair. "He changed his mind about that. He's singing a different song now."

"He is?"

"Yeah, as I recall he had a change of heart around about
the time I held his guitar out a second-story window. Plus, I
told him I wouldn't ever help him lug around his band
equipment again if he kept bothering you."

He ran a finger down the nape of my neck, which made
it very hard to do things—like concentrate on the conversation, and breathe.

"Do your parents know about all of this?" I asked.

"They overheard some of it, but they didn't say much.
They couldn't really because my grandmother was too busy
lecturing about how young men treated young women when
she was a girl. Opening doors. Holding chairs. That took
quite a while."

I considered this while Tanner slid even closer to me. If
Rick had decided not to sing "Dangerously Blonde," wouldn't
he have told Adrian about it? He would have told her he was

doing it for her and then Adrian would have triumphantly told me about it.

But that hadn't happened.

Then again, if Rick had told Tanner in front of his parents and grandmother that he wasn't going to sing the song, that meant something. Maybe I really didn't need to get up in front of everyone in a skating outfit and sing.

I should have felt relieved or hopeful, but I didn't. I realized with almost a shock, that even if Rick didn't sing "Dangerously Blonde," I still wanted to audition for *High School Idol*. I wanted to do it for me and I wanted to win.

When had that happened? When had I stopped mocking all of those people with singing ambitions and become one of them?

Tanner bent down and kissed me and I kissed him back. His arms felt warm and comfortable and for a few moments I didn't think of auditions, or Rick, or anything. There was just Tanner and me, and he was holding me close. It was enough.

Chapter 16

Friday brought rain, which immediately turned to ice, and then it snowed some more. This didn't mean that the football game would be canceled. Football players are too rugged for that, or fans too insistent, one of the two. What it did mean was that we got to wear our cheer sweats and gloves. It also meant, unfortunately that instead of riding in the school van with our advisor, we would ride in the school bus with the guys.

Moscow's high school is only a twenty-minute drive from PHS, but Mrs. Jones won't drive us anywhere if the roads are icy.

I don't mind riding to a game with the team, but trust me, riding back home with a bus full of riled-up, sweaty guys is not something anyone would voluntarily do.

The game started out well. The sky cleared, we scored a touchdown during the first ten minutes, and Mike got tackled. As if this wasn't enough to put me in a good mood, I noticed Naomi up in the stands flirting with Bjorne Jansen, a foreign exchange student from Sweden. He didn't speak much English, but Naomi's body language was easy to read in any language.

So much for, she understands me better.

That's one of the perks of being a cheerleader. You get to watch the crowd. Sometimes it's as entertaining as the game. I wondered how long it would take for this incident to get back to Mike.

Molly and Polly came, although they were barely distinguishable under their down coats, long scarves, and hats. They sat alone and as the stands filled up I kept checking to see if someone would sit next to them. But no one did.

Rick and some of his friends showed up, and Adrian arrived with some other sophomore girls, both of which surprised me since neither Rick or Adrian are football fans.

At first I was afraid they'd gravitate toward each other, talk, and work things out. But when Adrian saw Rick, she sent me a withering glare, as though she thought he'd come to see me.

Which was only true if he was looking for material for his follow-up CD: *More Reasons to Hate Cheerleaders*. The only attention he threw my way was the few times when he rolled his eyes at me.

We sang our song during halftime and it went perfectly. I loved the feeling of belting out the tune and knowing my voice did everything I wanted it to. High notes, low notes, I held onto them triumphantly. The crowd clapped and cheered, giving me an incredible rush. As I smiled up at the audience I thought, this is why Rick wants to sing for a living.

And I'm not sure which was a bigger compliment: that I noticed Mr. Metzerol in the stands, nodding in rhythm with the song—I knew he'd just come to see my performance—or that Rick stared down from the stands, absolutely stunned.

The only time he'd heard me sing before was the pep assembly when I did my impromptu duet with Mrs. Jones.

Yeah, I wanted to tell him. *I'm a little better with music, practice, and the help of my new best friend, Mr. Metzerol.*

As we walked off the field, Aubrie grabbed my arm. "We're totally going to kill the competition tomorrow."

"I hope so." I smiled and then remembered that Aubrie is the optimistic one. I turned to see Rachel's expression.

She nodded in agreement. "Rick is toast."

Samantha said, "All you have to do is sing for the judges like you just sang for this crowd. No pressure. No reason to be nervous."

But I wasn't. "I can do it," I said. "It feels like I've been waiting my whole life to do this and just didn't know it until now."

We didn't say any more about it after that because we'd reached the stands, but we all cheered extra loud for the next few minutes.

Rick didn't roll his eyes at me anymore. He only scowled. I could see him talking to his friends, spitting out words. He got up from his seat and wandered around the stands, talking to this clique and then to that. Networking, I supposed. Proving to me he could play the popularity game if he wanted.

Adrian left not long after that, probably to sulk. Which was stupid because Rick would have eventually gotten around to talking to her group.

We won the game 21 to 14, and the crowd started their

own impromptu cheer of: "We'll take state again!" Then the team, fans, and cheerleaders assembled on the edge of the field to hear the coach give his usual commentary/pep talk and to sing the fight song. After that, the fans headed back to their cars and the team to the bus.

Samantha and I took seats up at the front. We made it there long before Rachel and Aubrie because they were walking with some of the guys. The dating goddess was always in high form after a game.

I noticed Coach Davison talking to Mrs. Jones a little ways away from the bus, and neither looked happy. Then Bryce and Derek, two linebackers, rattled up the steps. Bryce shook his head at us. "You guys are busted. Someone ratted you out."

"What?" I asked.

"Someone told the coach you've got beer in your duffel bags," Derek said.

Samantha wrinkled her nose like it was a ridiculous thing to say, which it was. "We don't have beer in our duffel bags."

I didn't chime in to agree because I noticed Mrs. Jones and Coach Davison stop Rachel and Aubrie as they walked by. Coach Davison took their duffel bags from them.

"Look," I nudged Samantha and pointed to the scene out the window. "Someone is about to feel foolish."

That's when Coach Davison pulled a beer can from Rachel's bag. Both Aubrie and Rachel's mouths dropped open. So did mine. And then my heart pounded in my chest. I turned and grabbed my own duffel bag from underneath my seat. As I did, I noticed Coach Davison open Aubrie's bag and pull a can from it too. He gripped the can while Aubrie shook her head vigorously. She put her hand against her chest, protesting.

Coach Davison gave her a grim look and headed toward the bus.

I fumbled with the zipper on my duffel bag. The cold made my fingers clumsy. After long moments the zipper finally came open. There along with my make-up kit and granola bars lay a can of beer. "How did this get in here?" I breathed out.

Samantha had her own duffel bag open on her lap, and she glanced down at a beer can with horror. "We've been set up," she whispered. "We've got to get rid of these."

"Where?" I asked. The bus didn't have any hiding places, and I couldn't have pried open one of the windows if I'd wanted to. I glanced at it anyway. The coach and Mrs. Jones were almost to the bus steps.

Samantha grabbed the can from my duffel bag. I had no idea where she planned on hiding it. Before I could ask her, she put my can next to her own, zipped her bag shut, then shoved it back underneath her seat.

I stared at her. "What are you doing? They'll find them in your bag."

She took my bag, zipped it, and slid it underneath my seat. "Yeah, but they won't find anything in yours."

It still didn't make sense. She leaned toward me. "This has to be Rick's fault. If we're not students in good standing, we can't sing for *High School Idol*. This way at least you'll still be able to audition."

I didn't have time to answer. Coach Davison was beside

me, his gaze boring into mine. "Do you girls mind handing me your duffel bags?"

I glanced at Samantha and gulped. I felt my face flushing in frustration and anger. We pulled our bags out and handed them to Coach Davison. First he opened mine. He rummaged around the contents, then set it aside without comment. Then he opened Samantha's.

He immediately pulled out one of the cans of beer and held it up for Samantha to see. His jaw clenched tight. "Would you like to tell me what you're doing with this? You know the rules about alcohol at games. It's an automatic two-week suspension from school."

Samantha blinked up at him. I knew she was trying to look surprised but her words came out frightened. "I didn't put that there. Someone is trying to get us in trouble."

"Us?" he asked. "Who else has beer with them?"

She didn't answer. If we admitted that we saw what happened with Rachel and Aubrie, then they'd know we had time to rearrange the contents of our bags.

Coach Davison nodded at Samantha's silence. "I'd like you to step off the bus for a minute. We need to call your parents."

Samantha stood and pushed past me without another word.

 барбар барбар барбар

The ride home was horrible. Aubrie was near tears, Rachel was so steamed you could have boiled rice on her lap, and Samantha sat with a look of broken trust on her face. I don't know which reaction made me feel worse.

Even though I knew this was Rick's fault, part of me felt guilty about it anyway. They were in trouble. I wasn't. And they wouldn't have been in trouble if they hadn't been helping me in the first place.

Rachel told me every word Mrs. Jones and Coach Davison had said to them. Mrs. Jones had tried to stick up for the squad. "The duffel bags were by my seat, but I wasn't watching them that closely," she had told Coach Davison before he'd called everyone's parents. "It's possible that someone sneaked the cans into the duffel bags. The girls might be telling the truth."

"Might" was not a strong enough alibi to keep him from calling parents.

While he did, Mrs. Jones told Rachel, Aubrie, and Samantha, "We'll talk to the principal on Monday. I'll explain and hopefully she'll lift your suspension."

"Hopefully" was not all that comforting and Monday would be too late.

We discussed the situation in hushed voices on the bus ride home. "You could just sing with me anyway," I said. "We've already got the paperwork signed that says we're students in good standing. The judges won't know what happened tonight."

"You don't think Rick is going to tell them?" Rachel said. "If you win, he'll have you disqualified faster than you can say, 'sore loser.'"

"And what if the principal doesn't lift our suspension?" Aubrie asked. "They have evidence against us; it's just our word that we didn't do it."

"Mrs. Jones will help us. She believes we're innocent." Samantha cast a glance in our advisor's direction. "I think."

Rachel lowered her voice even further. "Mrs. Jones should have been watching our stuff better and none of this would have happened."

True, but I couldn't muster much anger at her. "She couldn't have known that Rick would do this." It hurt to say the words more than I thought it would. After all, I'd known Rick was my enemy. He'd never made a secret of it. So why had I thought that lately his complaints against me were more hype than hatred? Dating Tanner hadn't made me immune to this sort of attack.

"We can't let him get away with this," Rachel said.

Aubrie shook her head. "We have no way to prove it was him."

Rachel's eyes narrowed, calculating. "Is there any way to let the air out of his tires right before he has to leave for the auditions?"

"We need to concentrate on winning first. Then we'll worry about Rick." Samantha turned in her seat, surveying me. "You'll have to sing a different song. What's another one that you know the words to?"

Offhand I couldn't think of any. Besides, I hadn't practiced any other songs with Mr. Metzerol. I didn't know where to breathe and how to hold onto the notes or anything else. I'd only barely been able to get the notes of this song in the vicinity of my forehead. How could I start all over again and have something ready by tomorrow?

"I don't know what would work best with my voice. Plus

if I'm nervous, I won't be able to remember any of the words of a new song anyway. And what about dance moves?" The more I thought about it, the harder it seemed. It was a huge, insurmountable mountain. I couldn't do this alone.

Still, all the way back home we tossed out song titles. I even tried to sing a few of them to see if they were in my voice range. Nothing sounded good. Nothing.

I nearly forgot about the party. It only fluttered back into my consciousness when we pulled into the PHS parking lot. As we got off the bus Aubrie said, "There's no way my parents are going to let me go to Garret and Joe's party."

"Ditto," Rachel said, then looked over at me. "And you shouldn't go either, Chels. You've got work to do."

I nodded and we plodded toward our cars. While we walked my friends threw out more suggestions for me. I nodded at these too, even though they barely registered in my mind.

"We'll be at the auditions rooting for you," Rachel said. "Well, just as soon as we let the air out of Rick's tires." I was not sure whether she was joking about that or not.

"Thanks." The word came out of my mouth wavering. "You guys are great."

I noticed Logan coming across the parking lot. He'd been at the game, but of course had no way of knowing about the drama that had happened on the way back.

"Hi guys," he called cheerily. Then to Samantha he said, "Ready for *Pride and Prejudice*?"

And that's when Samantha's composure broke. She'd

been so collected on the way home that I'd thought she was okay. But as soon as he spoke to her, tears welled up in her eyes. She let out a little sob and threw her arms around him.

His arms tightened around her and his lips brushed against her hair. "What's wrong?"

"Rick planted beer cans in our duffel bags," I told him. "So I'm without back up singers for the audition tomorrow, and if Mrs. Jones can't convince the principal that the cans didn't belong to us, Samantha, Rachel, and Aubrie will be suspended for two weeks."

Logan stared back at us, stunned. "You're kidding."

"Nope," Aubrie said.

"We're going to let the air out of his tires tomorrow before he leaves for tryouts," Rachel added.

Logan shook his head, his expression serious. "No, you're not."

"Yes, we are," Samantha choked out.

He ran his hand across her back. "What about all of that stuff you said last year about taking the high road, and revenge not being the best way? Don't you believe that anymore?"

"Yes," she said, "but Rick can't keep walking over people."

"You're not going to do it," Logan said, but the softness in his voice made me unsure as to whether it was a command or a prediction. "You're not going to do something that's illegal just to get back at him."

She put her head back down on his shoulder and didn't answer.

The rest of us said our goodbyes, and we went our

separate ways. I drove home, fighting to keep the lump in my throat from transforming into a crying jag, and wondered if Mr. Metzerol took emergency phone calls.

Adrian wasn't home when I got home, and she hadn't left a note like Mom instructed, but that wasn't a surprise. I wouldn't let myself worry about her. I didn't have time.

I sat down in front of the computer to surf the net for possible songs.

It was hopeless, I knew, even before I logged on. A new song wouldn't solve my problems. I needed my backup singers back. I put down the mouse and picked up my phone.

Pacing across my room, I called Tanner. When he answered his phone I told him everything that had happened. "Can you make Rick confess to putting those cans in our duffel bags? If he confesses then my friends will be able to sing with me."

"You think Richard framed you?" I could hear the doubt in Tanner's voice, and I knew he didn't believe it.

"Yes," I said. "I think Rick would do anything to win."

There was a pause on the line and I could almost sense Tanner arranging his words. "Okay, sometimes Richard doesn't play by the rules, but he wouldn't stoop this low. He wouldn't get people suspended from school."

I gripped the phone harder than I needed too. "You haven't even talked to him yet and you're taking his side?" And that's when I realized it could never work out between Tanner and me. No matter what we'd said yesterday in the car about ignoring each other's siblings, we couldn't. As long as Rick and I didn't get along, Tanner would have to choose sides. And apparently his strongest loyalty would always be to his brother.

Tanner let out a sigh. "Look, I really don't think he had anything to do with it, but I'll talk to him and let you know."

We hung up, and while I waited for him to call back, I took off my cheerleading stuff, flung it onto the floor in a heap, and kicked it—I knew it was childish, but I'd stopped caring. Then I changed into my grubbiest sweats. Five minutes later he called me back. "Richard said—and this is a direct quote—that he doesn't know now, has never known, and never wants to know anything about the contents of the cheerleading squad's duffel bags."

"And you believed him?" It was a stupid question. Tanner had believed Rick before he'd even asked him about it. Still, it amazed me that Tanner could be so blind.

"Chelsea," Tanner's voice turned soft, reasoning. "Why would he risk getting you in trouble when he already thinks he's going to win? No offense, but Richard's been at this for years."

And apparently Tanner thought that meant no one else stood a chance.

I said, "I don't understand why Rick does the things he does. I guess that's always been part of the problem." My throat felt tight. It was getting harder to push out the words. "Look, Tanner, I've got to get off the phone. I need to figure out a new song for tomorrow."

"Chelsea . . ." He let out a sigh and didn't say anything else. Well, what else was there left to say? "I'll let you go then."

He was letting me go, I knew, in more than one way.

I shut my eyes and then opened them again. It was too easy to picture Tanner with my eyes closed and I didn't want to see him right now.

"Good luck with your audition tomorrow," he said.

"Thanks," I said, but didn't mean it.

Then we said good-bye. That part I meant.

After I hung up, I went back to the computer, fighting harder than ever to keep the tears at bay. Even with my eyes open I could see Tanner's face. I could see the way he'd smiled at me before we kissed. But I didn't have time to cry about this. I needed to stay angry. Anger was easier to deal with and more time-effective, too. Anger gave you energy. Tears just made you weak.

I was on my third music site when the doorbell rang. I trudged to the door and opened it, already resenting the interruption. Molly and Polly stood on my door step. "Hi, we called a little while ago, but it was busy." Polly's gaze took in my faded sweats. "We wanted to get your opinion on our outfits in case we needed to change before we left for the party."

Molly looked me up and down. "I told you we were overdressed."

Which made me feel even worse. They had put all that time into getting ready, and I'd been so upset about everything I'd completely forgotten to call them and cancel.

I invited them in, then explained what had happened. "I'm sorry, but I don't have time for the party. I've got to learn a whole new song."

"Why not just get new backup singers for your old song?" Molly asked.

"Because I don't know anyone else that can sing who isn't already trying out themselves." As soon as I said the words I realized I did. And they were standing right in front of me.

Chapter 17

I nearly gasped in excitement. "You guys could do it."

Polly gasped too, but not in excitement. "No, we can't."

"Mr. Metzerol says you have beautiful voices."

"And I get nosebleeds when I'm nervous," Polly said.

"So don't get nervous," I said.

Polly looked back at me like I'd just told her to stop breathing.

"We could do it," Molly told her sister. "It wouldn't take us any time to learn the song." Then to me she said, "But we're not doing any of those dance steps, so don't even ask."

"No dance steps," I said. "You can just step and clap or something."

"What were your backup singers wearing to audition?" Molly asked.

"A sparkly dress which may in fact be an ice skating uniform."

"We're not wearing those either," Molly said.

Polly raised her voice. "Did I mention that I get nosebleeds in front of crowds?"

"She has a point," I told Molly, "Maybe you should wear

football uniforms, like we did for the game. That way she can shove toilet paper up her nose and it will just look like it's part of the costume."

"Okay," Molly said. "We'll sing in football uniforms." She snapped her fingers. "We can put a cheat sheet on a football, just in case we have trouble with the words."

Polly folded her arms. "Do I have any say in this?"

Molly turned to her, with a stern look. "Chelsea is our friend and she needs our help."

She said this so simply, and yet it still hit me with eye-blinking force. With that one sentence I had been bestowed friendship status. They wanted to help me. I could see Polly's resistance melting as she considered her sister's words.

"Oh sure, guilt me into it. All right, I'll do it, but if the number is interrupted by paramedics rushing onto the stage because they think I've suffered some sort of head wound, don't blame me."

"You'll be fine," Molly said. To me she said, "She worries too much." Then Molly glanced back at her sister. "That reminds me, did you bring Kleenex for the party tonight?"

Polly patted her pants pocket. "Check." She patted her other pocket. "Check." Then she flipped open her purse. "And check."

"We're ready to go any time you are," Molly said.

"We'll go after we've practiced the song a few times." I didn't want to tell them what a perfectionist I was about practicing, for fear they would immediately take back both their offer of help and friendship. We would most likely not have time to go to the party, because we'd be practicing for hours.

But as it turned out, Molly and Polly picked up the song effortlessly. And Mr. Metzerol was right. They sang beautifully. I stopped worrying that they wouldn't get the number down and started worrying that they would out-sing me.

An hour later we were ready, for both the auditions and the party. I changed into jeans and a sweater, and then we left.

Cars lined Garret and Joe's street. From the looks of it a lot of people were here. As we walked toward the house, I gave Molly and Polly last-minute instructions. "Stick close to me. I'll try to find a time when Joe is alone and then I'll go up and ask him about something. After we've talked for a few minutes, Molly will ask me where the bathroom is, and I'll volunteer to show her. I'll tell you I'll be right back, but in fact I'll give you ten minutes alone. You can make conversation for ten minutes, right?"

Polly flipped open her purse and pulled out a piece of paper. "I made a list of things to say. I even jotted down notes about tonight's game."

"Great." I took the list and put in back in her purse. "But don't look at that list while Joe is around. You want to appear relaxed and confident, remember?"

"Relaxed," Polly repeated, "and confident."

We rung the doorbell and someone yelled, "Come in!"

I was about to, when I noticed Polly blinking repeatedly. "What's wrong?" I asked her.

"One of my contacts suddenly hurts."

"That's why sensible people wear glasses," Molly said. "They don't accidentally fold over in your eyelids."

Polly dabbed at her eye with a finger. "It will be okay in

a second." Neither Molly or I opened the door, though. We just watched Polly's eyelids fluttering.

Finally Polly turned to her sister. "Maybe it's not the contact. Do you see anything in my eye? A piece of dirt? An eyelash? A small crowbar?"

Polly held her eye wide open and Molly peered at it. "I don't see anything unusual except your mascara. It's starting to run."

That's when the front door swung open and Joe greeted us. "Hey, don't wait for an invitation, come"—his voice trailed off as he saw Polly blinking furiously—"inside."

"She's not winking at you," Molly said. "She's got contact problems."

"Contact problems?" Then Joe let out an "Ohhh," of understanding. "You mean contact lenses." He chuckled to himself. "For a second there I thought you meant physical contact."

Polly let out a strangled laugh and blinked harder.

Molly hurriedly said, "No, she doesn't have physical contact problems. She could make physical contact with you without any trouble at all."

Polly smacked her sister in the arm with one hand and covered her eye with the other. "Maybe I'd better go home."

I took Polly's arm and pulled her into the house. "I'm sure you can fix your contact in the bathroom."

We walked into the living room and immediately noticed people sprawled all over the couches and floors. Well, at least I noticed them. Polly with one hand over her eye apparently didn't notice much and nearly stepped on Mike's leg.

"Watch where you're going," he said, and then he saw me. His eyes narrowed as his gaze went back and forth between Polly and me, but he didn't say anything else.

Naomi wasn't with him, but I didn't have time to think about that piece of information. I put my hand on Polly's shoulder and propelled her toward the hallway, weaving her around people and objects. Molly followed close after us. "Hey," I heard a voice somewhere back in the room chide. "Do you have a license to drive that thing?"

I hoped that neither Molly or Polly heard this, or if they had, that they didn't realize that the comment was directed toward us. It had been a mistake to bring the twins here, I realized. It probably would have been okay if Aubrie and Rachel had come with us too, but at this point I was Ms. Dangerously Blonde, and my teetering popularity was apparently not enough to keep people from being rude.

Still, the only thing to do at this point was smile, pretend we belonged here, and only make an exit after it was clear no one had chased us away.

And perhaps that comment would be the worst of it. I mean, certainly as soon as Polly stopped flapping her eyelids like she was trying to take flight with them, we'd look like just another normal group of party guests.

We found the bathroom, and Molly and I waited outside while Polly fiddled with her contact. "I can't believe he answered the door," she said from inside. "And I can't believe you told him I'd have no trouble making physical contact with him."

"Sorry," Molly said. "I didn't come with a list of pre-pared topics like you did."

Polly's voice dropped to a growl. "Just don't say anything to anyone for the rest of the night."

"I didn't even want to come here," Molly hissed back. "You made me."

And then neither of them spoke until Polly emerged from the bathroom. "How do I look?" she asked me.

"Great," I said, and I wasn't lying. She looked nice. She was even standing with good posture. It was unfair that even though she looked so much better, stood so much more con-fidently, that someone had still made fun of her when she'd walked in.

What did people want from her? They'd tormented Molly and Polly for looking like geeks when they moved in, but now that they'd shaken off that image, people didn't want to treat them any better. Why did high school cliques have to be so rigid that once you'd been thrown in one, public opin-ion cemented to keep you there?

Well, it cemented to keep people at the bottom anyway. People at the top were fair game. We could be ripped off our pedestals at any moment. One misstep toward uncoolness and too many people were eager to see you topple.

"Come on," I said. "We'll get some sodas and mingle."

We walked to the kitchen and Molly followed us, arms folded and silent. I picked up sodas from an ice chest and handed one to each of the girls. Then I saw Joe by the sliding glass door and nodded in his direction. "Let's go."

Polly whimpered, but followed after me. Molly still didn't say anything, and I wondered if she planned on being sullen all night. That would make mingling a lot of fun.

We reached Joe. He'd apparently just put a dog outside and was still gazing in that direction. A layer of white covered the lawn, and his golden retriever was sniffing around, making a trail of gray circles in the snow.

"Hi Joe," I said.

"Hi Joe," Polly said.

Joe looked at me, not at Polly. "Hey, sorry to hear the cheerleading squad got in trouble tonight. No one on the team believes you guys are guilty."

"Thanks," I said.

"Of course, that doesn't mean we won't razz you about it anyway."

"Thanks," I said. This was just what I wanted to hear.

I glanced over at Polly. She wore a look of pained nervousness. I tried to change the subject to something she could join in about. "You guys played a great game tonight."

"We did okay," Joe said.

Polly smiled eagerly in his direction. "I saw you running down the field, you know, the time when that other guy ran over you."

Joe grimaced. "That describes a lot of times."

"And I saw them all." Polly sent her sister a look and I could tell she was waiting for Molly to ask me something, so I had an excuse to leave Polly alone with Joe.

Molly just pressed her lips together and looked around the room.

Polly turned her attention back to Joe. "I thought you played really well."

"Yeah," I added, and tried to think up an excuse that would take Molly and me away. I needed her help with . . . um . . . what?

"I bet if you hadn't dropped the ball that time, you would have made a touchdown," Polly said.

Joe sent her a stiff smile. "Funny—the coach told me the exact same thing—except his veins popped out of his neck while he said it."

"Oh." Polly, immediately grew distressed. "I didn't mean to imply that you'd messed up the inning."

"Play," he said, because innings are in baseball, not football.

Polly looked at him blankly. "What?"

"Play," he said again. "First down."

"Down?" Her eyes grew wide. Then she looked at the floor. "Exactly what are we playing?"

I elbowed her. "He's not giving you an instruction, Polly. He's talking about the football game."

"Oh, right," she said. "I knew that. English is my first language."

"Speaking of English," I said, "weren't you telling me about a study group you wanted to put together for English class?"

"Yeah." Polly put hand to her nose like she was smelling her knuckles, only she didn't move her hand away.

Joe shrugged. "I could use some extra help in English."

"Great," Polly said. "I mean great that you want help, not great that you're bad at English." She still didn't move her hand. It meant that she'd either gotten a bloody nose or was afraid of getting one.

This is not the way a girl wants a guy to remember her. You said hi, you flirted, and then you bled all over his carpet.

I tried to think of something, anything I could do to help. "Hey, what a great ceiling you have." I looked up intently, as though admiring the beige paint. So did Polly and Joe. This at least would keep Polly's face tilted in the right direction.

"My ceiling?" Joe repeated.

"Cool light fixtures too," I said. "Are your light fixtures the same in the hallway?"

"Uh, no, they're in the wall."

I grabbed Polly by the arm. "Let's go check." Partially because I wanted both hands free to guide Polly, and partially because I wanted a reason to come back and talk to Joe, I thrust my soda can into his hands. "Could you hold this for me for a minute?" Before he had a chance to answer, I turned and propelled Polly toward the hallway. Molly followed behind us, shaking her head.

I led Polly through the room and she kept her head tilted upwards the entire time. "Wouldn't this room look great with crown molding?" I said, as we walked by a crowd.

"And a mural of clouds," she answered.

As soon as we got to the hallway that led to the bathroom, Polly retrieved her Kleenex from her pocket and held it to her nose. "That was awful," she said. "Joe must think I'm totally strange now."

"Not at all," Molly said. "I'm sure a lot of girls ask him about playing on the floor and then spontaneously bleed."

Glaring at her sister, Polly pulled the second wad of Kleenex from her pocket and held it to her face. "You wanted me to look like a fool, didn't you?" She stormed into the bathroom, and shut the door. I heard the lock click and then the sound of crying.

I tapped softly on the door. "It's not that bad. I was the one who started talking about the ceiling. If he thinks anyone is strange, it's me."

No answer except for sniffling.

Molly ran her hand through her hair, sighed, and leaned against the door. "I'm sorry. Will you come out now? Joe is probably wondering what you were going to tell him about the study group."

And what to do with my soda can.

Polly's voice came out muffled. "My nose is bleeding, and I can't face anyone."

"All right," Molly said, "I'll face them for you."

The door opened and for a moment I caught site of Polly, a huge wad of toilet paper crammed against her face, then Molly slipped into the bathroom and the door closed again.

I supposed that Molly was in there giving Polly a pep talk, or applying pressure or something; I wandered further away from the door, looking at the family photos on the wall while I wondered how to salvage the meeting with Joe.

"So did you ditch Tweedledee and Tweedledum?"

I turned and saw Mike, leaning up against the wall where the hall emptied into the family room. He held a drink loosely in one hand and his gaze traveled over me in a way that Naomi wouldn't approve of.

I bristled at his comment, but smiled at him anyway. "I notice your girlfriend isn't here. Was she afraid to come to a place where calories might leap out at her?"

Mike took a sip from his drink, then turned his attention back to me. "Naomi and I broke up this morning."

Which explained her performance with Bjorne at the game. "Oh, sorry," I said, because it must hurt to get dumped for a guy who barely speaks English.

One eyebrow lifted and his eyes studied me. "Are you sorry? I sort of thought you'd be glad."

I shrugged. "Well, okay, a part of me thinks you deserved to be dumped, but I was too polite to mention it."

He rolled his eyes. "I broke up with her, Chels. I admit it—you were right—she only has three topics of conversation and two of those are about herself."

"Oh." I didn't feel happy, just vindicated. "I thought she understood you."

"I guess I didn't understand myself." He stepped over to my part of the hallway and leaned against the wall next to me. "I wasn't seeing things clearly, but I can still see it was a mistake for us to break up."

He said this as though it had just occurred by itself. As though we were walking through school one day and—poof—we weren't a couple anymore.

But it hadn't happened that way. He'd decided that he liked someone better than me, and he'd thrown everything we'd had away. Now he just wanted me to forget about all of that?

I leaned away from him. "Well, what's done is done."

"But that doesn't mean it can't be undone." He took another step toward me. "Look, I know it's been really hard on you. I know that's why you've been acting this way."

"Acting what way?"

He shrugged as though it should be obvious. "The Chelsea I knew would never drink beer while cheering for a game."

Just the reminder made my stomach clench. "I wasn't drinking at the game."

"Your bag was the only one that didn't have a beer can in it. Why was that?"

For a moment I couldn't say anything. All the words rushed to my mouth at the same time and tangled themselves around my tongue. How could he know me and just assume I'd been drinking? He knew I never drank. My father's drinking had made my childhood miserable and I didn't want anything to do with it. Mike and I had had this conversation when we'd dated. Had he forgotten? Or had he never really listened to me in the first place?

"None of those cans were ours." I said. "Rick framed us so we wouldn't be able to audition for *High School Idol*."

"If it was Rick, wouldn't he have put something in your duffel bag too? You're his main competition."

I clamped down on the words that wanted to stream out of my mouth. If I admitted that Samantha had taken the can out of my bag and it got back to the coach, I'd be in the same trouble as the rest of the squad.

"It was Rick," I said.

"And do you blame Rick for making you hang out with the Patterson twins, too?"

I lowered my voice to a near whisper. "There is nothing wrong with the Patterson twins."

"Nothing wrong if you want a membership to the Loser-of-the-Month Club. Look, I know you've made them your little project and you gave them makeovers and everything." He held up one hand as though conceding the point. "I'm not saying you didn't do a good job. They look better, but they're never going to matter to anyone but you. They're dead weight, Chelsea, and they're dragging you down. People are talking about it." He put his hand on my shoulder, gently massaging it. "You need to cut them loose and hang out with real people."

The horrible thing was I knew what he said was true. People were talking. Molly and Polly weren't helping my social standing. And they probably would never matter to anyone at school but me and a few others. It was true, and awful, and unfair in a way that stung my insides.

I looked up at Mike and kept my voice even. "Remember when you told me that Naomi understood you better?"

Perhaps he could feel the rigidness in my muscles because his hand moved from my shoulder to my neck, still massaging. "I'm sorry about that."

"No, you were right. She must have understood you better, because I didn't understand you at all." I took his hand and moved it off my neck. "But now I do, and I don't like what I understand."

He let out a sigh. "I know you're upset about Naomi—"

"This isn't about Naomi," I said. "It's about Molly and Polly. What kind of person refers to other people as dead weight?"

"A realistic one."

The bathroom door opened and Polly stepped out. She motioned in my direction. "Chelsea, can you come here for a second?"

I sent Mike a stiff smile. "I've got to go." Then I walked back to Polly.

"How do I look?" she asked. "Does anything look out of place?"

I examined her face. I saw no signs of blood or telltale signs of crying. She didn't even have red eyes. I glanced over her clothes to check for stray drops of blood but didn't see those either. "You look fine, amazingly fine."

She leaned closer to me. "That's because I'm Molly. We switched clothes in the bathroom. We figured if you couldn't tell the difference no one else would."

I looked behind her for Polly, but apparently she had no plans of emerging from the bathroom. "What did you do that for?"

"So I could go make small talk with Joe, and he'd still think she was a normal person." She smoothed out her sweater and shook her head. "This is so awkward."

"Because you don't want to flirt with Joe?"

"Because I can't see. I had to give Polly my glasses to hold."

I put my hand to my face. "Maybe this isn't a good idea."

"Really, Juliet?"

What could I say after that?

Molly adjusted the bottom of her sweater. "I couldn't possibly be worse at flirting than Polly was. Besides, we've done this before. After the party, I'll just tell her everything

Joe said to me, and he'll never be the wiser." Molly ran her hand through her hair, fluffing it. "I think Polly should go out on a limb and really lay on the charm, don't you? I mean, what's the point of liking a guy if you're too shy to let him know?"

I glanced back at the bathroom door. "I don't think Polly would want you to do anything drastic."

"Just point me in the right direction. Which one of the tall blurs is Joe?"

I stepped out into the family room with Molly. Mike was still there, lingering near the hallway. He saw me scanning the room and walked up. "Who are you looking for?"

"Joe has my drink," I said.

"I can get you another one." Mike took a step toward the kitchen, but I called after him.

"You don't have to do that. Polly can go get it."

Mike glanced in the direction of the sliding glass door. "Joe might be in the back yard. Garret was showing some girls how his dog retrieves snowballs—oh, there he is."

I looked and noticed Joe pulling open the door for a group of people to go outside. "He's by the sliding glass door," I told Molly.

"Okay," She put her shoulders back, the exact same pos-ture that Polly had adopted lately, and strode across the family room.

Joe and the group stepped out onto the patio and shut the door. The group went out onto the lawn, but Joe stayed next to the door. Perfect. Molly would be able to talk to him alone.

As though Mike had read my mind, he leaned closer to

me. "Don't you think you're carrying this project of yours too far? Joe is way out of her league. You'll only make him feel uncomfortable and make her feel stupid."

I tore my gaze away from Molly long enough to glare at Mike. "Molly is smart and funny and any guy should be flattered to talk to her."

"I thought that was Polly."

"It is, and Polly is just as wonderful and smart as—"

I heard a crash from across the room and my gaze swung back in that direction. Molly lay on the floor, blinking in surprise and confusion.

Mike took a slow sip of his drink. "Yeah, real smart. Your friend just walked into the sliding glass door."

Chapter 18

Cringing, Molly sat up and held her hand to her nose. I rushed over, but before I'd reached her, Joe opened the door and stepped inside. "Are you okay?" he asked.

Molly gathered herself and stood up. "I'm fine. I just didn't see the door."

"Is your nose okay?" I asked, because she hadn't moved her hand away from it.

"Um . . . I think it's bleeding."

Oh, if Aubrie had been here, she would have been all over the irony.

"Here," Joe took her by the elbow, "I'll show you to the bathroom." They walked, and I followed after them. Mike followed after me. I'm not sure why. Maybe to gloat.

Of course the bathroom door was locked. After Joe knocked, we heard Polly's voice, worried, say, "I'll be out in a minute."

"Can you hurry?" Joe asked. "Polly has a bloody nose."

Which must have been a strange thing for Polly to hear. She cracked open the door, and I could see her—a wad of

Kleenex still held to her nose—peering out at us. "How did you . . ." Her voice trailed off as she saw Molly.

Joe did a double take when he saw Polly holding tissue to her face. "What happened to you?"

I let out a gasp which even in my own ears sounded forced. "It's one of those mystic twin phenomena! Polly got hurt and so Molly's nose started bleeding. Amazing!"

And everyone agreed that it was amazing, especially Polly who said the word while glaring at her sister.

We left the party after that. I'm glad to report that we left with our heads held high, even if it was, in part, because two of us didn't want to bleed on the carpet.

In the car on the way home, Polly sat beside me while Molly lay down on the backseat. Polly drummed her fingers against the armrest and slowly said, "I can't believe that while you were dressed as me, you ran into a sliding glass door."

"I couldn't see," Molly said.

"Well even a blind person could have noticed that there weren't gusts of cold air wafting in front of them. That should have signaled to you that the door was closed."

Molly let out an exasperated grunt. "Sorry, I was too busy thinking of what to say to the guy you liked to monitor the weather."

"I'll never live this down," Polly moaned. "At school I'll be known as A+ Polly again."

"Well, then just be glad our blood type isn't B negative," Molly flung back, "since that fits you better."

In all the time I'd known the twins, this night was the first time I'd heard them argue. It was my fault, since none of it would have happened if I hadn't brought them to this stupid party. I shouldn't have, just like I shouldn't have made them hope that things could be different for them in high school.

"I can't even make it through a party," Polly said, sniffling. "How am I going to make it through auditions tomorrow?"

No one said anything for a moment and maybe we were all thinking that the audition was doomed. Finally I said, "What those people at that party think about you doesn't matter, so don't let them upset you." I knew I wasn't just saying it to her. I was saying it to myself because there was a very real chance that Rick would win the *High School Idol* spot, become a rock star, and torment me with anti-Chelsea smash hits for the rest of my life. I couldn't let it matter anymore.

〜 〜 〜

I checked Adrian's room when I got home. She was in bed, lights off, sleeping. The sight relieved me, not just because she was home but because while she lay there serenely, makeup off, she seemed like the sister I used to get along with. It reminded me that the old Adrian was still there, somewhere. I turned from the room, touched the doorknob and then tapped the edge of the door three times.

I lay in bed for a long time thinking about auditions. I made a mental checklist of everything I needed to take tomorrow, even though I'd left most of it sitting in a pile by my bedroom door. I'd taken my mother's alarm clock and put it next to mine just to ensure I wouldn't sleep in.

I didn't need to worry. I swear I woke up every hour to check on the time. When morning came, I pulled myself out of bed feeling more exhausted then when I'd laid down.

Still I rushed around getting ready, doing my scales as I did. I threw on a pair of faded jeans and a Cougars sweatshirt. I was not about to walk into the auditorium wearing my sparkly outfit. Professionals, I was sure, changed when they got there.

Mom called at 8:15 in the morning to wish me luck. I walked into the garage at 8:30 to put my stuff in the trunk and found out that Adrian had taken the car. I especially appreciated this since Adrian wasn't supposed to drive anywhere and she knew I needed the car to get to Beasley coliseum on campus for the auditions. I called her cell phone. She didn't answer. Then I called Molly in a panic, but luckily they hadn't left yet and could swing by and pick me up. By 8:55 we walked up to the registration desk. We were supposed to be there by 8:45 even though auditions didn't start until nine.

The lady at the desk didn't seem to notice or care that we were late. She didn't even ask to see proof that Molly and Polly were students in good standing, something we were prepared to do with a phone call to the school's guidance counselor. She just handed me a packet of information and a large white tag that read #63, then had me check off my group's name on her list.

About a hundred names filled the roster. I didn't recognize a lot of them. They must be kids from Moscow and other neighboring towns. After we'd finished signing stuff, she told us to wait outside in the hallway for our number to be called.

"But we're sixty-third in line?" I asked. "So how long will it be until they call us?"

She gave me a cold stare, like I should already know, or at least like it was impertinent to ask. "The average audition is three minutes, but sometimes it goes much faster and if you miss your call, that's it. We won't audition you later. That's why we ask that all of the contestants stay in the hallway and not leave the premises."

"Thanks." I turned away, mentally doing the math.

Molly had it figured out before I did. "About three hours," she said. "It's a good thing I brought a book."

Three hours? Why had they told us to be here so early, and why hadn't I thought to bring something, anything to do?

I recognized several kids from Pullman milling around in the hallway—some in regular clothes, some decked out like rock stars, but I didn't see Rick. As a professional, apparently he already knew that you didn't have to be here on time.

It would have served him right if he had been the first up, but no, while a thin man with a goatee welcomed us to auditions and gave us directions, I looked around and found the first ten contestants. They'd already pinned their numbers to their shirts. After goatee guy had finished emphasizing that we needed to get on and off stage as quickly as possible, he took the first ten contestants backstage to wait in the wings.

Molly, Polly, and I found a corner and went over our routine a few times. Then there was nothing else to do but wait and listen to the strains of music floating into the hallway.

I hadn't realized when the registration lady told me that the auditions averaged three minutes, what she meant was that if the judges didn't like you, they only gave you about thirty seconds to sing. If they liked you, they let you go on for a minute or two. The extra minute was spent ushering people on and off the stage. I learned this from the contestants who straggled back into the hallway, and told us in varying degrees of worry, how far they'd gotten into their song.

"I've been practicing my routine for a month. My whole family came out to see me, and I didn't even make it to the chorus," one girl said. "It was totally unfair."

"See," I whispered to Polly like this was a good thing, "It will be over so fast, your nose won't have time to bleed."

I heard Rick before I saw him. His voice carried down the hallway in a clipped rhythm. "Well, isn't it just convenient then, that you were there to lug my equipment around."

"I didn't do it," Tanner said. I recognized his voice too. In fact my heart paused for several seconds at the sound of it. Something that shouldn't happen.

I heard the sound of footsteps and knew Rick and Tanner were about to round the corner. "I told you I wouldn't sing the song," Rick said. "But that wasn't enough, was it?"

"I didn't do it," Tanner said again.

And then they were walking toward the rest of us. Rick carried his guitar case in one hand while clutching a paper that read eighty-six. Tanner carried a boom box. Neither one saw me, and I knew I ought to turn my gaze to something else and pretend I didn't see them either. But I couldn't keep my eyes off of Tanner. Dark hair, square jaw, piercing blue eyes . . . I'd stop staring at him in a second. In another second. In another second.

He turned and caught my eye. I looked back at Polly, who was watching me with one eyebrow lifted. "Aren't you going to go say hi to him?" she whispered.

I hadn't told anyone about my phone call with Tanner last night. I just shook my head and tried to maintain a normal heart beat. Tanner's presence shouldn't fluster me. I'd just keep looking at Polly. He'd be gone in a second.

"Chelsea." His voice made me jump. I hadn't heard him walk over, but he stood beside me, still holding the boom box. Rick glared at me but followed him over.

I plastered on a smile. "Hi, Tanner." Then through gritted teeth I added, "Rick."

Tanner shifted the boom box under one of his arms. His gaze trained in on mine, and there was a tightness about his eyes. "Rick woke up this morning to find the air let out of the tires on his and my parents' cars. You wouldn't know anything about that, would you?"

Surprise kept me from answering right away. I mean, sure my friends had talked about it, but I didn't think they'd do it. And how had they gotten inside of Rick's garage anyway?

I shrugged in Rick's direction. "I don't know, have never known, and never want to know anything about the air pressure in your cars' tires."

His head moved, like he wasn't sure whether to nod or shake his head, and he held out a finger in my direction. "I didn't put anything in your stupid duffel bags."

"Then we both have clean consciences, don't we?"

Tanner stepped between us. "Great. I'm glad you guys

got a chance to straighten that out. Where do you want me to put your stuff, Richard?"

"Anywhere." Rick broke off from glaring at me to take in his surroundings. He waved to a place further down the hallway. "How about there."

Without another word, Tanner walked over and set the boom box down by the wall. Rick turned back to me. "I'm going to guard my stuff now, but in case you're wondering, I've got my guitar, my boom box, three CDs of background music"—he patted his jacket pocket—"and my iPod with speakers. There is no way you can sabotage my song."

I smiled back at him. "Has anyone told you that you're paranoid?"

"I'm prepared. Are you?" Rick sent me one last scowl and went off to guard his stuff.

Molly and Polly peered after him. "I think he has issues," Molly said.

"Should we have brought extra CDs of our backup music?" Polly asked, and her voice had the beginnings of panic.

"He's just trying to psyche us out," I said. "Besides, I have an extra copy of our background music in with my clothes." After all, I hadn't sung an a cappella duet with Mrs. Jones and learned nothing.

With his hands tucked into his pockets, Tanner walked back over to our group. Molly saw him coming, took hold of her bag and said, "Come on, Polly. Let's change into our football gear." Before she left, she paused, leaned in close to me and whispered, "I know he's your boyfriend, but don't take your eyes off of our background music for a second."

Paranoia, apparently, was catching.

The twins headed toward the restroom, which left me nothing to do but watch Tanner walk up.

"Hey," he said. "I just wanted to wish you good luck. Break a leg. Preferably not Richard's leg, though."

I knew he was trying to make me laugh but I couldn't muster much more than a smile.

Tanner glanced back at his brother. "Richard can't bring himself to ask you, but he really wants to know if Adrian is here."

"I'm not sure where she is. She'd already left with the car this morning when I got up. So Rick wasn't the only one who had to hitch a ride here."

Tanner's eyebrows lifted and disapproval sprung into his voice. "Adrian left you without a car?"

"Yeah, it's nice to have my family's support." I shrugged as though it didn't bother me, but Tanner didn't notice. He looked past me, his mind somewhere else.

"She won't talk to Richard," he said after a moment. "He's called and left messages but she won't return them. Why is she so upset?" He let the question linger in the air. I could tell he was trying to figure everything out, and I suddenly felt what I'd done was inexcusable. How could I explain to Tanner that I'd kept Adrian in the dark about Rick and me to protect her from him?

"When was the last time you talked to her?" he asked.

"I checked on her last night when I came in."

"But when was the last time you talked to her—said more than a few words in passing?"

"I don't know. She hasn't said much to me since she broke up with Rick."

He nodded as though this too was part of the puzzle, and I had to stifle the urge to spill everything. Why was it that Tanner did this to me? One well-placed look into my eyes and I would have turned over my diary and let him read the whole thing.

"Have you tried calling her to see where she is?"

"She didn't pick up."

"Maybe she will, if I call. What's her number?"

I gave him the number. If I hadn't, Rick would have.

"I'll let you know if I find anything out," he said. Then he wished me luck again and walked back down the hallway toward the auditorium doors.

Molly and Polly came out of the restroom dressed in football jerseys and sat on the floor again. I decided I'd wait until the goatee guy took more contestants backstage before I changed into my sparkly outfit. I didn't want to sweat in it. I recited the words to my song, chanting them like it was a prayer.

I could do this. I had an advantage over most of these people because I was used to performing in front of crowds. I performed at every pep assembly and game.

So yeah, Rick, who says cheerleading is a useless skill?

I wandered around talking to other people in the hallway, all the while keeping an eye on Rick. He sat by his stuff, listening to his iPod, and mouthing the words to whatever he was listening to. Curiosity propelled me in his direction, and I walked close by him, pretending I wanted a drink from the drinking fountain.

I recognized the music coming from his iPod. How could I not? It was the background music for "Dangerously Blonde."

So much for Rick's deal with his brother.

At ten-thirty, the judges took a break. They had to, because crushing all those dreams is strenuous work. Goatee guy came into the hallway, tapped his watch, and told us we had ten minutes before he took the next group of contestants backstage.

Rachel, Aubrie, and Samantha came to find me. They all gave me hugs. "The judges are going to love you," Samantha said.

"Yeah, because the rest of the numbers stink," Rachel said. "We've heard so many cracking voices you'd think they were serving helium back here."

Which is what jitters do to most voices and another reason I was glad I'd already sung in front of crowds.

Samantha let out a sigh. "I wish we could be up there with you."

"I'm almost glad we're not," Aubrie said. "I'd be so nervous." She immediately looked like she wanted to take back the words. "Not that you should be nervous, because you'll do great."

"Thanks." I leaned in closer and lowered my voice. "I can't believe you guys let out the air of Rick's tires."

Samantha's head tilted. "What? We didn't do that."

I thought she was joking. "You really shouldn't have," I whispered. "You could have gotten in a lot of trouble if you'd been caught."

Rachel shook her head. "We didn't do it."

My gaze went back and forth between my friends, waiting for a smirk that would let me know they were lying. But they didn't smirk. "Then who did?"

Rachel shrugged. "Either an enemy of his or a fan of good music. They're both large categories."

Aubrie looked past Rachel and down the hallway. "Well, whoever did it, it didn't stop Rick for long. There he is."

"That doesn't matter," Samantha said. "All that matters now is what you can do on stage. And Chelsea, you can do it."

This statement was followed by several others along the same lines. They said they'd all come visit me in L.A. once I became a big star. Rachel made me promise that I'd introduce her to Orlando Bloom.

She might have requested a few other invitations as well, but Samantha glanced down the hallway and said, "There's Tanner."

Rachel's gaze flickered over to him. "Do you want us to stay or do you want time alone with him?"

Samantha didn't give me time to answer. "We're going. Trust me, when Tanner is around, you don't want to try and keep track of the verbal camouflage Chelsea throws around."

They wished me good luck again, and left.

Even before Tanner reached me, I could see the seriousness in his expression. It wasn't just in his eyes. It was in his walk, his posture. His gaze met mine, but he didn't smile.

I knew the look. I'd seen it before. It was the look of condolence people wear before they deal you a blow.

At first I didn't understand. I thought, well, he's going to give me some sort of talk where he officially says we shouldn't see each other anymore. Not much of a surprise, so it shouldn't hurt.

It shouldn't, but it still did. Each footstep he took down the hall bruised me.

And then I saw the open cell phone in his hand. It wasn't about us, I realized, it was about Adrian, and it wasn't good news. Even before he spoke, my heart stopped. Something horrible had happened.

Chapter 19

He held the phone out to me, hesitating. He didn't want to do this. It's a car crash, I thought with panic, just don't let her be dead.

"Adrian wants to talk to you," he said.

Good. She was alive. I took the phone from his hand but my hand shook. "Adrian, where are you?"

Her voice came across the line, ragged with emotion. "I'm in Spokane."

Which was way better than being in a hospital, but still, Spokane was an hour-and-a-half drive away—not a place a person with a learner's permit should go by herself. "What are you doing in Spokane?" I asked.

"I have a flight out at 1:00. I'm going to live with Dad."

Several seconds went by before I could speak then I sputtered out, "What? You can't do that." The worry pumped through me harder, because I knew she could. She shouldn't. But she could. He had joint custody.

I stepped away from Tanner to give myself privacy, to think.

"Dad said I could come anytime, and I think it would be best—" Her voice broke off.

"You don't think that," I said, because she couldn't. She knew what Dad was like as well as I did. I pressed the phone to my cheek, willing Adrian to be logical. "Turn around and come home. If you're leaving because you think I'm interested in Rick, you've got it all wrong. I went out with Tanner a couple of times. That's why his car showed up at our house. That's why Rick was talking to me at my locker."

She cut me off as though she hadn't heard me. "I know what I saw. Guys start out liking me but end up liking you. I'm just not enough for anybody. They all want to move on to Chelsea, the deluxe model."

I shut my eyes, trying to make all of this undo itself. "I promise you there is absolutely nothing between us."

"Maybe you believe that. Maybe you don't think about things until after they've 'just happened.'"

"Or maybe I'm telling you the truth."

"You're only making me feel worse for what I did." Her voice broke again. She didn't finish.

"What did you do?" I asked but I'd already guessed. She'd let the air out of Rick's tires. He'd forgive her easily enough, though. After all, he'd been asking for her. He wanted her here. My mind was already sprinting into the future, already bringing Adrian home. I turned so that I faced down the hallway toward where Rick sat. In a moment I'd walk over and hand him the phone so that he could assure her that none of it mattered.

"I put the beer into your duffel bags."

The future skidded to a halt and I was suddenly back in the present. "You what?"

"It wasn't fair, Chelsea. You always get what you want."

Her voice was not accusing now, just sinking, and asking me to understand. "It doesn't matter for most things, but music is all that Rick ever wanted. He's worked his whole life to succeed at it. I couldn't let you just waltz in and take that away from him on a whim. I'm sorry I got you and your friends suspended. I'll call the principal on Monday and confess."

It only vaguely registered in my mind that she didn't know I wasn't suspended. I gripped the phone, shocked. It had been my own sister. Tanner had told me that Rick wouldn't sink that low, but Adrian had. My thoughts spun around the betrayal; dark, black, and swirling with anger. It was an unforgivable act, worse than anything I did to her with Travis.

But my fury died as quickly as it flared up. It's hard to stay mad at a person when moments earlier your heart stopped beating in fear of her death.

And besides, my amazement seemed bigger, more solid than the anger. She'd done this for Rick. They weren't even going out anymore. She had thought he'd betrayed her in the ultimate way—by liking me—and yet she still cared enough about him to want to hand him his dream.

She had told me, but I hadn't believed her. She really did love him.

"Chelsea, are you still there?"

"Yeah, and I still want you to come home."

I heard her take a ragged breath. "I can't. I've ruined everything with you, and with Rick, and I just need to go away for a while."

"No, you don't—"

"I'm sorry." Then silence. I checked the cell phone, but

even before I saw the "call ended" sign, I knew she'd hung up.

I stared at the phone, my thoughts racing.

Tanner walked up. "Is she coming back home?"

I shook my head.

"Can you get a hold of your mother?"

I punched in her number, and waited, but she didn't answer. "I don't know what she could do anyway," I said as the phone rang. "She's in Arizona."

Mom's answering message came on. Her voice sounded so happy in it. It could, because she didn't realize she'd just lost one of her daughters. I told her to call me right away. Before I'd even hung up the phone, I walked over to Rick. Tanner followed me.

When I reached Rick, he looked up at me suspiciously, "What do you want?"

"Your help."

He shut his eyes and leaned back against the wall. "Sorry, last time I checked hell hadn't frozen over."

"It's about Adrian."

His eyes opened but he still regarded me suspiciously. His gaze darted over to his brother and then back to me. "What about Adrian?"

"She's at the airport in Spokane. She wants to go live with our dad because she thinks she's messed things up here too badly." I shoved the phone at him. "Call her. Tell her to come back home. She'll listen to you."

"What?" Rick's eyebrows drew together, like he didn't quite believe me. "Why did she leave?"

"She put the beer in the squad's duffel bags."

Instead of using Tanner's phone, Rick pulled out his own, and pressed Adrian's number into it. He glanced back at me while he waited for it to connect. "Why did she do that?"

"Because she wanted to make sure you won the audition."

"And she didn't think I could beat you? That's a nice vote of confidence." As he held the phone to his ear, his hand tapped against his jeans. "So she'll be suspended. It's not the end of the world. There are worse things."

"Like living with my dad," I said.

Tanner and I watched Rick silently, waiting for a sign that Adrian had answered.

But Rick let out a grunt and shook his head. "She's not picking up." To her voice mail he said, "Adrian, don't get on the plane, okay? Just call me." He shut the phone and hit redial. I watched him while my insides slowly fell to my feet. She wasn't going to answer. She wasn't going to come home.

Rick stood up, agitated. "So much for 'she'll listen to you.' She won't even talk to me." He swore then, although I assume not into her voice mail. He shut his phone and called again. "It doesn't make sense. Why would she sabotage your song so I'd win, and then take off so I never see her again?"

It hurt to admit it, but I had to. "Well, she sort of thinks you have a crush on me."

"She what?" Rick said this too loudly, and several people stared in our direction. "Just because I was at your locker on Tuesday?"

"That, plus she saw Tanner take me home on Monday and thought it was you." Both Tanner and Rick stared at me, so I quickly added, "I told her she was wrong. I told her I'd never done anything to make you like me."

Rick hit the redial button. "That's the truth and then some."

While Rick paced around the floor cursing, Tanner continued to stare at me, his gaze heavy. I could tell he knew what I'd done. I took a step closer to him and lowered my voice. "I did tell Adrian there was nothing going on between Rick and me."

"But you didn't prove it to her. That would have been easy enough. All you would have had to do was tell her to talk to me."

"I thought it was better if they didn't get back together." When his eyes turned accusing, I added, "You said as much yourself when I went to dinner at your house. You were glad that Rick and Adrian had broken up."

He let out a sigh and his gaze traveled past me, to where Rick paced across the hallway with the phone. "He's been calling and leaving messages for her for the last two days, asking her to come to the auditions. He cares about her. So my opinion doesn't matter."

I looked over at Rick. "And she cares about him." Saying it made me feel worse. Adrian cared about him and I'd messed things up for her. Again.

Rick walked over to us, shoving the phone back into his pocket. "Tanner, I need your car keys."

"Why?" he asked.

"I'm going to the airport to talk to her."

Tanner's head tilted back. "Right now? In the middle of auditions?"

"It will be too late afterward. The flight leaves at 1:00."

"How do you know that?" Tanner asked.

"I called the airlines. There's only one direct flight to Chicago." Rick looked at me then, but without the anger I'd expected. There was only bitter resignation. "I guess you'll win after all. Let me be the first to congratulate you."

I shook my head. "No. You stay here and finish the audition. I'll drive to Spokane and talk to her."

Rick snorted. "You already talked to her, and nothing you said made her want to come back. I'm going."

Tanner glanced back and forth at us. "You can't go to the gate to talk to her without a ticket."

"So I'll buy one," Rick said.

I only had a few dollar bills in my wallet, and I didn't own a credit card. Still, I wasn't about to let Rick win on this point. "I'll tell the airport people she's running away from home. They'll have to stop her. Rick can stay here and audition. I'll go."

"I'm going," Rick said.

"Fine, then we'll both go," I said.

Tanner held up his hands. "Neither one of you have a car, and I'm not letting either of you tear up the highway to Spokane in mine. Besides," he said as he pulled his keys from his pocket, "you'd kill each other before you reached the airport. I'll drive."

"Let's go then," Rick turned, and picked up his equipment. He handed some of it to Tanner to carry.

I ran over to Molly and Polly to let them know I was leaving. "You can withdraw from the auditions if you want. Or you can just do it without me."

They both stared at me over their books, wide-eyed. "We're backup singers," Molly said. "How would we do the song without you?"

"One of you could take my part." I didn't wait for their reaction to that suggestion because Rick was already striding toward the door and I didn't want Tanner and him to leave without me. I grabbed my purse but left everything else with the twins. Then I ran to catch up with the guys.

∽ ∽ ∽

I sat next to Tanner in the front seat of his car while Rick leaned over the back seat and complained about Tanner's driving.

"Man, that light was almost yellow. You could have gone through it."

I glanced over my shoulder at Rick. "I'm surprised you're still alive."

Rick grunted. "I'm a good driver."

"I don't think she meant that," Tanner said tightly. "She meant she was surprised I haven't killed you yet. Keep telling me how to drive and you might not be so lucky."

Rick sat back in his seat with a thud. "We've got to get there before they board. At this rate it will take forever."

"We'll get there in time if the roads are clear," Tanner said.

The roads were clear, and once we got out on the highway,

Tanner drove fast enough that even Rick couldn't complain. The rolling Palouse Hills zoomed by.

Tanner made Rick call their mother and explain the situation. She didn't pick up the call. They knew she wouldn't. The judges had instructed the audience to turn off their cell phones.

It was just as well, because neither Tanner nor Rick wanted to talk to anyone in their family anyway. They'd had a five-minute conversation beforehand about who should be the one to break it to their grandmother that her grandsons had taken the only car without flats and left everyone stranded at the auditorium.

But when Rick didn't show up on stage, they would check their cell phones.

It was a long drive, made longer by the fact that Rick kept tapping his door handle as though this would make the car go faster. Tanner hardly said anything. I could tell he was angry. It showed in the set of his jaw, in his grip on the steering wheel, and in the silence that surrounded him. I wasn't sure who he was angry at, but figured it was me. I didn't bring it up though. That wasn't a conversation I wanted to have in front of Rick. Besides I couldn't stop thinking about Adrian living with my father.

I watched the snow-covered hills and my mind flashed back to a winter night, one of the last we'd had before my mother left him for good. She was at work and Dad was supposed to drive us to a Christmas program at church. He stopped at a bar instead. There we were, in dresses and tights—Adrian just six years old, and I was eight. He said he'd only be a few minutes and left us in the car. We waited for a while, shivering in the cold, but I knew he'd be in there all night so I took Adrian's hand and we walked home in the snow. It was miles, and Adrian cried all the way because her pretty shoes were getting wet and ruined.

Dad didn't come home until hours later, but when he did he slapped me across the face for disobeying him. When Adrian shrieked in protest he slapped her too.

When we were twenty miles away, Mrs. Debrock called Rick's cell phone. He told her why he was heading to Spokane, reiterating all the reasons he'd already given her in his message. He grunted and rolled his eyes at whatever her response was. After he'd slid the phone back into his pocket he said, "Grandmother thinks I'm undependable, impulsive, and unable to see things through to the end."

Tanner looked straight ahead at the road. "I'm sure she'll cool down by the time we get home, but if not, hey, more of an inheritance for me."

I turned so I could see into the back seat. "You're being dependable—dependable for Adrian. That's something that's worth seeing through to the end. Your grandmother will realize that one day."

Rick didn't answer for a moment. He just stared at me like he didn't know how to react to my compliment. Finally, he looked out the window and shrugged. "Maybe," he said.

After that, we spent a few minutes planning what we would do when we got to the airport. Rick would buy a ticket and go talk to Adrian alone. I agreed to this only because I didn't have the money for a ticket. If he couldn't convince Adrian not to get on the plane, then he'd call me, and I'd tell the airport authorities that she was running away from home. We saved that option for last, because we didn't want to get Adrian in trouble if we didn't have to.

When we pulled up to the airport parking garage, my stomach was churning. The clock in the car read. 12:10. Her plane would probably start boarding in twenty minutes. How long would it take us to get to the gate? As we got out of the car, Rick carried his boom box with him. "Why are you taking that?" Tanner asked, but Rick didn't answer and there wasn't time to discuss it. We jogged into the airport.

Tanner and I went and stood in the ticket line, which was a dozen people long. Rick walked to the counter and told the agent he needed to buy a ticket *right then* because it was an emergency. She cast him an unimpressed stare and told him he'd have to wait his turn.

He swore about this, and continued to swear all the way to the back of the line. Really, the boy needed to expand his vocabulary.

"Would you be quiet," I hissed to him, "I'll handle this." I turned to the man who stood in front of us, tapped him on the shoulder, and gave him a damsel-in-distress smile. "Excuse me, sir, but my little sister is trying to fly to Chicago when she shouldn't. We need to buy a ticket so we can go back to the gate and keep her from getting on the plane. Can we cut in front of you?"

He stepped aside immediately. "Sure thing, honey."

I repeated this plea all the way up through the line, and one by one the customers let us through until we reached the front of the line. After I'd thanked everyone profusely, I turned to Rick. "See," I whispered. "It pays to be polite."

"You mean it pays to be a leggy blonde," he whispered back. "They wouldn't have done that for me."

"Just think of it as a cheerleader in action," I said.

He shook his head and didn't reply.

We watched the agents, waiting for one to become available and my stomach resumed its churning. I took hold of Rick's arm to get his attention. "Tell Adrian I'm sorry we fought, and I should have told her about Tanner earlier, and I just want her to come home."

He kept his gaze fastened forward, ready to step away from me. "Okay."

"And tell her Mom will be miserable if she leaves."

"Okay."

"Tell her that she'll never be happy at Dad's and—"

"Chelsea." Rick put one hand on my shoulder to quiet me. His voice turned soothing. I'd never heard it that way before, and it reminded me of Tanner. "I can handle this. I'm going to bring Adrian back, okay?"

I gulped and nodded. "Okay."

The agent called Rick to the desk. While I watched him pull out his wallet, it hit me more forcefully what Rick was doing—what he he'd done already. "I can't believe he left the audition for Adrian," I said.

Tanner's voice was hard. "I can't believe she sabotaged your song for him."

"Now your grandmother won't help him."

"Now your school will suspend her."

"Yeah, it's like some Goth version of Romeo and Juliet, isn't it?"

He laughed but I could see the tenseness around his eyes. We were still apart, the two of us. The day hadn't changed that, and I wasn't sure why. Everything else had changed so quickly. I'd started out with Rick as my archenemy and now somehow we were on the same team.

"I guess Rick isn't so bad underneath all that grungy black clothing," I said.

He glanced at me to see whether I meant it. I must have looked sincere because he smiled cautiously. "Yeah, he has his good points."

"I probably could try harder to get along with him," I said.

"Good." Tanner looked at the airline counter not at me. I waited for him to say something else. He didn't.

"This is where you say, 'And Adrian isn't so bad either.'"

The muscles around his jaw line twitched, and I realized that his anger was directed toward her and not me. He shook his head. "She made both you and Richard miss your auditions."

"She didn't make us; we chose to leave."

"She tried to get you suspended so you couldn't compete. How can you just forgive her for something like that?"

I didn't answer for a moment. I wasn't sure I had forgiven her; I hadn't consciously done it, anyway. I just knew that despite all the ways and all the times Adrian and I had hurt each other over the last couple years none of it had mattered when I thought about losing her. "She's my sister," I said.

Rick turned around and called to me, "Hey, Chelsea. The agent needs to see your driver's license."

I stepped up to him, already getting it out of my purse. "Why?"

"Because I'm buying you a ticket too. I think we have a better chance if we both talk to her." Before I'd thought about it, he took the license from my hand and gave it to the agent. "Don't worry," he said with a glance at my face. "I'm buying refundable tickets. You won't owe me anything."

While the agent looked at my license Rick added, "Unless we apply the fare to a different trip. Maybe we should fly to L.A. and hit the auditions there."

We didn't have time to discuss it because the next moment the agent handed us our tickets and we rushed off through the airport corridors toward the security checkpoint.

Rick, by the way, moved pretty fast for someone who's biggest mode of exercise so far had consisted of skulking around school. Tanner wasn't even out of breath as he ran and I mentally noted what good shape he was in. Lacrosse must do that for you. I struggled to keep up with them.

When we reached the security checkpoint, I stood there panting and surveyed the line. It looked like at least a twenty-minute wait.

Rick nudged me and nodded at the people in line. "Time to turn on the blonde. See if you can move us ahead any."

One by one I explained the situation to the people in front of us. "Please sir, we have to reach my sister before she boards the plane."

I felt like the teenage version of Tiny Tim, but everyone let us through. We reached the front of the line where you had to show your boarding pass to a screener. I ought to have turned around, given one last, God bless you everyone, to the people behind us, but instead Rick and I hurried through it and ran to the gate.

The line had already formed to board the plane and Adrian stood in it, staring ahead with vacant eyes. She hadn't done her hair or makeup and she looked young, tired, and afraid. I knew my father was in Chicago, but it felt like he stood on the other side of that door, and once Adrian stepped across it, he would never let her go again.

She saw us and her eyes flew wide. "What are you doing here? You're supposed to be at auditions."

I walked to her, breathless, wanting to hug her but afraid she'd push me away. "We left because you're more important to us," I said. "No matter what happens, your home is here with Mom and me, and it was Tanner—I'm crazy about Tanner, okay? I don't like Rick at all."

Rick nodded. "And I don't like Chelsea."

She looked back and forth between the two of us hopefully. "You still hate each other?"

"Yes," we both proclaimed cheerfully. Then we glanced at each other.

"Well, I mean, he's okay as *your* boyfriend," I said.

"And I guess I don't mind her dating Tanner," Rick said, "but you have to know that you and I . . . well, you and I . . ." He took her hand and pulled her out of the line. "Here, sit down. I want you to listen to this."

Then right there at the gate, he turned on his boom box and sang to her. The music was to "Dangerously Blonde," but instead of those lyrics, he sang,

Adrian, let me start
To tell you the way I feel.
Though others try to stop us,
You are my ideal.
I'm dangerously in love.

We shouldn't fight, girl,
It isn't right, girl,
Letting them tell us what to do.
Believe in me and I'll worship you.
I'm dangerously in love.

There was more of it, all just as cheesy; which goes to show you there is a reason why rebellious-fringe guys don't generally write love songs. But Adrian started crying after the first verse and didn't let up until Rick finished and she'd thrown her arms around him. Everyone at the gate clapped for them and tears I didn't even realize I had ran down my cheeks.

When she let go of Rick she turned to me and hugged me. "I'm so sorry," she said.

I said, "I'm sorry too." And then both of us cried harder, but it felt good because finally things were right between us.

After a minute I said, "Let's go home," and then the three of us walked back toward the security area, Adrian and Rick holding hands.

When we got to Tanner, Adrian blinked in surprise and said, "You came too?" and then before anyone could say anything she tilted her head as though she should have known beforehand and said, "That's right, you and Chelsea . . . they told me." She leaned in toward him confidingly and added, "I'm glad that she's crazy about you. You guys make a great couple." Then she and Rick walked on, absorbed in each other, while Tanner watched me with one eyebrow raised.

He didn't comment right then, although as he followed after Rick and Adrian I could tell that he was considering what she'd just said. I didn't say anything. I mean what does one say after that? Yes, I really am crazy about you. So tell me, are you still interested in me at all?

Rachel said guys got scared away if you acted needy. What happened when a girl called a guy and accused his brother of framing her, then got mad at him for taking his brother's side, when it had been her sister all along? Rachel never covered that topic, but I figured the results would not be good.

By the time we reached the parking lot, I needed to say something, anything to anyone, just so I wouldn't blurt out something to Tanner that I'd immediately regret. To Rick I said, "Hey, I really like the new version of your song. Are you going to rewrite the rest of those cheerleading songs? Because that would be so romantic to have the whole album dedicated to Adrian."

Adrian looked at him brightly.

"Sure." Rick put his arm around Adrian and pulled her in to a walking hug, but over her head he looked at me and said, "You are so manipulative."

I blinked back at him innocently. "And it got us to the front of the airport lines, so don't knock it."

Tanner let out a sigh. "No fighting, you two. From now on you get along, agreed?" He looked at Rick and then me, waiting for an answer.

"Okay," I said. "No more arguing."

Rick shrugged and held up one hand in surrender. "Okay."

Adrian leaned over so she could see past me to Tanner. "Thank you. The way they get sometimes—it drives me insane."

"Tell me about it." Then Tanner exchanged a look with Adrian that said he understood her suffering. It was like they'd bonded over the issue of how hard it was to deal with us.

I looked at Rick and rolled my eyes. Rick nodded in agreement.

Chapter 20

I probably should have driven our car home with Adrian and let Tanner drive his car home with Rick. But I didn't. When Rick suggested that he drive Adrian back in our car, I said, "Okay, just as long as you drive the speed limit and stop when the light is yellow."

"You're arguing with me," Rick said.

"No, I'm trying to save our car and your life."

He let out a grunt. "Fine. I'll stop when the light is yellow."

I didn't press the point because I wanted time alone with Tanner to talk. And we did. On the way back we talked about everything, everything but us. I wish guys came with maps like they have in malls. The kind that show the insides of the building, point an arrow to the spot, and proclaim, "You are here." It seemed like we'd been through so much that I had no idea where I stood when it came to him.

When we'd almost reached Pullman, my mom called me. She'd already called Adrian so she knew what had happened, but she still wanted to hear about it from me. I answered her questions, and told her that everything would be okay, be-cause even though Adrian would be in trouble with the school, at least she was happy, wanted to live with us, and no longer hated me.

Mom made a few more comments about that, and then in an almost after thought said, "And let me get this straight—you're dating Rick's brother now?"

"Tanner's not at all like Rick," I told her. "The entire time I've known him his hair has been the same color."

Tanner sent me a sideways glance and smiled. Mom told me we'd discuss it later.

When we were entering Pullman, Molly called me. It was hard to hear her because there was so much noise in the background. I kept saying, "What?" and finally I heard Molly say, "Polly, will you calm down, I'm trying to tell Chelsea that . . . oh yes . . . we won the spot!" And then there was more screaming both from Molly and Polly.

"That's great," I said, and okay, I did feel a twinge of jealousy. Actually, more than a twinge, a slap, really. But still, I was happy for them. "I knew you guys could do it."

Polly took the phone from her sister. "I didn't even get a nosebleed. And guess who was in the audience, and stayed after to congratulate me, and then spent like fifteen minutes talking to me and said we definitely had to get together to study?"

"Joe?"

"Yes, but only after he could get through all the other people who came to talk to me." She let out a happy breath. "This must be what it feels like to be cool."

"You are cool," I said.

"I am now. We just spent the last hour talking with reporters. I've got to hang up because our parents are taking us out to celebrate, but I wanted to ask you—you'll help us pick out clothes for our trip to California, won't you?"

"Of course," I said, and immediately outfits, complete with handbags and sleek pumps, paraded through my mind.

She told me that they hadn't known what to do with my stuff so they'd given it to Samantha. I asked Tanner if he could take me there to pick it up. I figured he'd just drop me off, but he parked the car and followed me to Samantha's doorstep.

Samantha opened the door and gave me a quick hug. "Molly told me what happened. Are you okay? Did you find Adrian? Here, come inside."

I didn't know which question to answer first so I sat down on the couch and told them everything—from Adrian's confession about the beer cans to the way Rick said he'd rewrite the words on his *Cheerleaders in Action* CD.

Rachel was the most upset about the beer cans. "We could have been up there on stage today. We could have won the slot."

"Except that Molly and Polly sing way better than any of us," Aubrie said. "We might not have won if it had just been us."

Samantha shrugged. "I bet if they become really famous they'll introduce us to all sorts of important people. Chelsea will be hired by some swank fashion designer, Aubrie will star on a reality show about gymnasts, and Rachel will date all the guys who starred in *Lord of the Rings*."

"Stop trying to make me feel better," Rachel said. "Half of the guys in that cast are too old for me."

Logan leaned back against the couch cushions. "Rick is

Janette Rallison

rewriting all of the words on his CD? I sort of liked the 'This Skirt Means I'm Too Good for You' song. It was catchy."

Samantha smacked him. The rest of us ignored him.

"But who let the air out of Rick's tires?" Aubrie asked. "If it wasn't us, and it wasn't Adrian, then who did it?"

Logan let out a small cough. It wasn't loud, but it was enough. All of us turned and looked at him.

"Logan?" I asked. "Do you know anything about it?"

He only shrugged. "I'm not saying anything with Tanner sitting right here—except that you guys should really be more careful about keeping your garage door locked."

Samantha turned to Logan, her mouth open. "You told me not to do it. You told me to take the high road."

"And aren't you glad you did? Don't you feel better now? I feel bad, but at least you don't have to."

Samantha continued to stare at him.

Logan shrugged again. "Okay, I don't feel that bad. The guy has been bothering my girlfriend, he deserved a few flat tires."

Tanner held up one hand. "I'm just going to pretend I didn't hear any of this."

I nodded in Logan's direction. "Maybe you should volunteer to help Rick reinflate his jeep."

"I imagine by now the jeep is already reinflated," Tanner said.

"Well then," I said trying to smooth things over. "I guess all's well that ends well."

Rachel humphed. "It won't end well until I get to meet Orlando Bloom."

We talked for a little while longer and then Tanner took me home. When we pulled up to my house he turned off the car but didn't get out. Instead he looked at me thoughtfully. "So, do you still believe in second chances? Although actually, in our case, I think we're on about our third or fourth chance."

"Probably," I said. "But I believe in those too."

"Good," he said. "So do I."

If he'd asked at that point, I would have also professed a belief in the tooth fairy and leprechauns. With him looking at me so intently, I could believe in anything. "How about fifth and sixth chances? I'm not trying to be pessimistic, but with Adrian and Rick as our siblings . . ."

"Good point," he said. "I definitely believe in sixth chances."

He said it so seriously that I laughed. "I don't think things will be *that* bad between Rick and me anymore. My opinion of him has gone up."

He nodded. "And my opinion of Adrian is way up."

Considering the things he said about her in the airport, this was news. "When did that happen?"

He looked upward, as though contemplating and his smile took on a mocking tilt. "About the time she said you were crazy about me, and I realized she hadn't ruined everything between us after all."

"Oh." I felt the beginnings of a blush and fought it.

His gaze turned to mine, still teasing. "It's probably for the best. I wasn't having any luck forgetting about you." He shrugged. "Mostly because I didn't want to." His hand slipped over mine and our fingers intertwined. "So I guess it's not such a bad thing Adrian ruined your audition. Otherwise you might have won and then you'd go to L.A. and meet all sorts of famous people."

"Yeah, that would be horrible," I said.

"It would be horrible for me." He smiled in a way that made me tingle. "Still, it's too bad you never got to sing your song." He tilted his head, surveying me. "You could copy Richard and sing your audition song to me."

"Sorry, I don't perform in cars."

"What song were you going to sing, anyway?"

" 'It's in His Kiss.' "

His eyebrows crinkled. He'd apparently never heard of the song. "What's in his kiss?"

"That's how you know if he loves you so."

"You can tell that from a kiss?"

"According to Cher."

"I never knew girls had that power." He pulled me closer and leaned down. "What can you tell from this?" Then he kissed me.

I should have thought of something to tell him, some witty retort about what his kiss revealed, but to tell you the truth, as soon as his lips touched mine, my mind stopped working. I'm not even sure how much time went by. Then a bang on the window jarred the silence. I looked over and saw Rick and Adrian outside the car staring down at us.

Rick shook his head in mock disapproval. "You'd think the two of you would set a better example for us, your younger siblings."

"I'm shocked," Adrian said. Then the two of them laughed and walked up the driveway and disappeared inside my house.

I watched them go and then turned back to Tanner. "Do you want to go inside? Rick and Adrian will probably give us no end of grief."

"I know," Tanner said. "Let's take them on together," and he held my hand again.